T0196158

Plot

Plot

a genre study

Wain Ewing

ARCHWAY
PUBLISHING

Archway Publishing books may be ordered through booksellers or by contacting:

Archway Publishing
1663 Liberty Drive
Bloomington, IN 47403
www.archwaypublishing.com
1 (888) 242-5904

Acknowledgements: "goback4" appeared in *The Alchemist*; "Pluck," "Escape from the Dome," and "Transport" in *Anemone Sidecar*; and "Boxed" and "Near Miss (Very Becoming)" in *Grasslimb*.

ISBN: 978-1-4808-6113-8 (sc)
ISBN: 978-1-4808-6114-5 (e)

Library of Congress Control Number: 2018904226

Print information available on the last page.

Archway Publishing rev. date: 09/04/2018

CHAPTERS IN SEQUENCE

goback4

The prisoner without a syllable or numeral
cracks open his own blind mess
with a rusty mallet.
Later is put to work
digging a canal.

Tonight over snowbound blue Rockies
the family zeppelin
returns to place-of-birth.
A wash of brass-colored light
issues from the windows of a snow-flurried gondola.

Though I return in chaos.
I remain.
And proceed.
The same direction.
An empty rowboat
poised on black waters
drifts below the falls.
Oars dangle through sleeves of sky.

Xpendable

I approach a shallow waterfall; a drop of four or five feet. Wearing "shit-kickers"--clunky tree-planting boots--why is it I must stand down with other "Xpendables" along the rocky shore?

Below the falls I attempt to balance on slippy stones just beneath the surface. Although my attention has begun to wander, I momentarily scan figures who seem to be making giant strides across the top from the "opposite shore."

Pluck

In the first or second row of this theater, I sit captive with the audience, in a full house. The curtains are drawn. The show soon to begin. In the interim, as I strum my duocello, the audience of albino ants responds with enthusiasm. I happen to note the thick flat pick with which I have been playing. When was it I made a pick like that before?

The foot race, I recollect, had three participants. Unhelpful (Brother), Disillusioned (Journalist), and me, voice-over.

Unhelpful had stopped to instruct a group of school children who sat at his feet...He is always humerous; they sort of like him, but he treats everything as a joke, is easily distracted, and they begin to see through him...Next, Disillusioned (Journalist) stops to speak to an attractive young woman in a strapless bathing suit. He attempts to persuade her that she smells bad, which recalls that time Unhelpful suggested a bottle of ink I had on my t a b l e smelled like shit. In f a c t the ink smelled like library paste. Last, I approach the same woman. Her hair is parted to one side and her nose is pointed like the duocello pick. It takes a lot to convince her that--although she sweats--she doesn't smell bad.

Sort Without Ilk

The School for 1 stage is smaller even than

JV gym stage. On a folding chair, still within the captive audience, I watch a man perform. He is on stage before he leaps off, hits the deck, and is gone. We see green glowing bones of his x-rayed skeleton fall writhing to the floor. All that is understood regarding his performance is: "He turned from a depiction of landscape to the stage."

Uncomfortable within the absence of precedent, contrariwise, in 101 Auditorium, I face the seated audience of which I am no longer a member. The stage itself is now behind me. 101 Auditorium is a good deal larger than JV gym…I'm near the edge where a prompter's box used to be, but instead of of facing toward the stage, I face outward toward the audience…Somebody has seen to it that there is no longer a captive audience. Not spellbound. Unenthralled, seated to my right, beside myself, is Unhelpful Bro who could still be…somebody else.

On stage, near its edge, a cossack with knife clamped between his teeth, hunkers down on his left haunch and begins to spin, "inscribing a circle," as in a 1920s Soviet film…With arms folded, tanked on vodka, he would make this hopping spin the finale of his drunken dance. As he spins with right leg stuck straight out, his felt-lined boot grazes the twinned necks: of me & of Unhelpful beside me. The moment the boot grazes his neck, Unhelpful starts away; I remain seated. I say to him, "No, don't. If you let that boot graze your neck, it could help you to think about things you need to be thinking about."

On reexamining the Auditorium, I see that the audience has been displaced by stage curtains, parting to reveal an outline of

landscape.

Boxed

At night, all the way back in Construe, my place of birth, I am walking up S. Ave. and then across toward B. Blvd. Finally, I turn right into an unfamiliar cross street, parallel to S. Ave., and am about to cut across a backyard to return to the Ave. when I notice an enormous boxer looking toward me. It is the boxer of an earlier drawing magnified ten feet tall. When it approaches I am afraid it will attack. However, I begin talking to the animal which--it turns out--is friendly.

I pat the creature.

In the same neighborhood, near Echoing Robot Garage, close to an unfamiliar cross street, I encounter a very pretty tall French woman with long chestnut-colored hair and rounded cheek bones who refers to me as "lamia" and asks where I live. I think of telling her I am living in the church before admitting, "I have a small room."

It is the other room, useful for eliminating endlessly digressive explanations.

So...I am going forward with "the other" when I split from him to goback4 a clear plastic box containing 1) antique little magazines? 2)  the sweater I gave her? 3) almost stale vegetables from the refrigerator? He proceeds without me. Not alone, I am in the room looking for a transparent box which I cannot find, though I look everywhere for it, since it contains me.

Traveling on a diagonal I pass through the city center where I discover an old tarpaper church. A passer-by suggests I ought to tell my real mother about the church.

Getting practical, for once, I make a concerted effort to locate the school which is neither of space or time, which I have labeled "School for 1." Although I know it is no building, I enter a building and walk around to discover if this could be it. I see that the lower part of the walls is painted a dark institutional color. The upper part is light color. I hear children before I see them walking single file in the halls …

Kindergarten basement classroom. The child is rather pleased, proud he has managed to get my attention. But when he clings I move to the right…At the bottom of those kindergarten stairs I remember a 6ft wooden box which contained a huge roll of brown paper used for group projects. I used to dream of being solid and enormous, buried alive inside that box, petrified, unable to move, which is not the case today. Today the box opens and I am able to move around. Formula: just as the School is not the building, childlike can never = childish.

To continue my research, I must float over arid terrain in a hang glider/ultralight which has sprouted a green rubber wing taut with helium. My boots crunch down momentarily on a crumbly-sandy mountaintop before I spring forward into the air …

Escape from the Dome

A nuclear station…of some sort. Either a power station or a depot for nuclear waste. The dome shape is shiny metal. Inside it 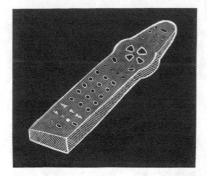 are corridors I tour with the group. Sort of, the ramp scene from Fritz Lang's *Metropolis*. A meltdown or explosion is immanent. Klaxons wail. We've got to flee. Everyone rushes forward, emerging into a sunlit field outside. I stand in the near distance looking back at the dome. Our carpenter's son as a nearly mute, bashful child appears to my right.

Many Gospels

Foreign Language Student tells me he, too, lived in Chinatown, though a different Chinatown, and probably for different reasons. This worries me, as though he might somehow try to recontextualize the invisible tatoo which is my history. Surely there must be an element he cannot recontextualize.

Although I by no means identify, I see him projected inside my 8 1/2 x 11 room in  Chinatown. A discussion ensues with mi madre regarding camera lucida and the window...I want her to know my history but have to accept that at her age she is never going to be particularly curious.

So, how does the establishing shot establish? And what if there were no one to repeat anecdotes?...What development could I hope to purchase in projecting FLS? Now I remember clearly...It was the day he said, "You sure got a lot of gospels." Smarter than me & with a head for foreign languages.

Multiplicity, the Faux Plea for Zero Tollerance

In Test Market 7, a long preamble proves not worthy of recall…on S Avenue, facing north… different Quag I era associates still hang out.

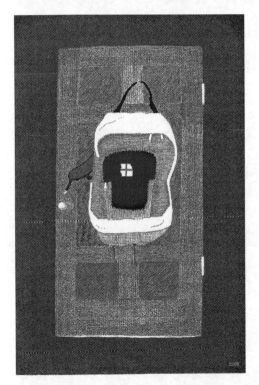

Tour group clear now except for Disillusioned Journalist. We walk north together on S Avenue in an area near Olde Tyme Farmer Market. Not much traffic at this hour, few pedestrians…I observe a door inset in a recently sandblasted brick wall…a finished wooden door you'd expect to find between rooms inside the house…We pass through this door …

Inside the building opens into a vast theater filled with row upon row of Japanese megacorp employees who've assembled for an important conference.

While I gape at the oceanic assemblage of salarymen and uniformed workers, Disillusioned, off to one side, confronts the Japanese captains of industry. I hear him speaking boldly to them, trying to get across his point; which is that there are far too many cooking oils on the market today. You have your peanut oil, corn oil, canola, rape seed, olive, safflower, sesame, plain lard, etc., etc. Too many oils…too many gospels. Also an excess of logos and brands…If 1 kult is ever gonna precede all other denominations, there can and must be only the 1 available at your corner market today…As in olde command-style economies, Disillusioned has developed an energetic plan to sweep all superfluous oils crashing from their shelves to have just 1 pure oil available 4all …

Transport

With Unhelpful I reenter an airy rooming house. Because the house is ablaze, our stay must be of limited duration. We climb a burning staircase to the second floor to enter a room. In it is my own desk. As though "fired" I am to sort through the desk drawer, selecting whatever is worth keeping before the room is engulfed in flames and we are assigned to departure. In the top, right-hand drawer are rolled-up tubes of what, on removing the caps, appears to be pimple cream, a flesh-colored ointment. I pitch these items into a wastebasket. But in another drawer I discover several small pocket knives which seem worth keeping. One has a brightly-colored handle.

At the student desk, filling out course cards, I begin to speak with the tenured professor

23

standing near who resembles a shrink. I begin to write down English and history for my courses but he suggests I ought to consider going back4 subjects in which I have as yet displayed only a thin proficiency. I flip the

jack knives at an archery target in a renewed, albeit somewhat futile, effort to please Obeys-her-Friends…(Both misses.)

Riding a bus across the border, heading for town, I converse with a prisoner beside me. We share some word with a third in the seat just in front, who had a jeweled clip. As we cross the border into town, I remark on mesas visible through bus windows…Meanwhile my word stash is transfered to the seat mate. Inside the bus station we have disembarked and the vague one won't return belief.

Instead, he hands my stash to a woman…In the bus depot, she inhabits a square, 3-sided plywood booth.

The Jonah Booth

"And the Lord said, 'Do you do well to be angry?'"
--Jonah 4.4

A couple of summers back my cousin and his two boys, ages three and five, and I, made a pilgrimage through the woods to an old tree house that no one visits much these days... In total, around three quarters of a mile out and back...We took turns pushing an empty wheelbarrow along the narrow woodland path, estimating that the boys would be tired before we completed our circuit and would need to be carried partway …

After the tree house, after turning over some rocks along the shore, where crawfish used to be found in abundance, my cousin hoisted his three-year-old onto his shoulders while I followed along behind, pushing the older one in the wheelbarrow.

Near the spot where the trail breaks through onto a gravel road, we stopped for a rest inside a walless pump house that once enclosed my deceased uncle's water pump back in the days when our drinking water was drawn cold in buckets, before uncle's well went sour. When his well had to be sealed, he hoisted the shed onto a pickup for removal to its present dusty resting place alongside the gravel road.

The four of us sat sweating on a bench around the inside with the wheelbarrow parked outside. It was dusty, close, rustic, not all that picturesque. As the boys shouted and flung stones, I alone of the 4 was old enough to recognize a glass peanut butter mug still hanging from a rusty nail, which brought to mind icy water, the distant sunshine of departed summers, also the vanished prospect from uncle's well.

Once we were ready to resume our hike, my cousin and I and the older of the two boys got up to go. However the younger son, who was feeling reluctant, remained inside the booth, staring out at us without speaking as we walked on ahead, some of us calling back to him, gently, mockingly …

"Don't you want to be left behind?"…But he was complacent and preferred to stay as he was, so he didn't cry out even when, at last, my somewhat exasperated cousin walked back to pick him up.

Well Hooked

In a lake boat with brunette, younger. She fishes, at last hooks into 1 good-sized. As before, the boat is an oceangoing craft launched into a fresh water lake. She fishes out the bottom. There is an opening in the hull, sort of a glass bottom boat, without glass, opening directly into the water …

With a big aluminium hook she snags a 2 foot fish through its lip. Not so well hooked. She is trying to land it before she transfers the line to me. I am supposed to land it. She requires this of me. I think the fish ought to be better hooked or no one will land it; it'll flip free, tearing metal through its lip. I allow the hook to sink down further inside before I give a tug and know the fish is hooked. I start to haul our catch into the boat but when I look again the fish has changed; it is large now and shark-shaped. I observe flat teeth; before it resembled more of a pickerel. The fish is hooked in its craw; the line…a thick noodle of string. I'm trying to get fish into boat, hauling it in through the frame in the bottom.

I've yet to land it when everything goes black …

Rice Jungle

Again I approach the resort…of some sort… Rice Jungle Resort. As I approach it, I notice a woman backing into a parking space in her vehicle of green plastic. A lot of ground cover has sprouted near where her car is parked. I don't go into the building but walk around to our car.

Father stands outside the vehicle as I open the door to remove a camera. Not a cardboard returnable this time, but a large

instrument with bulky lens attachment. (A lot of equipment.) Unlike Unhelpful Bro, father has no intention of making a snap. I hand father the

camera, saying, "In case you want to take a picture." He doesn't.

I move away from the vehicle and resort toward an athletic building in the distance with a playing field on my right. The field is green

and yellow in the sun. A few students can be seen kicking a soccer ball around. Without sighing, I have understood that Foreign Language Student can now probably afford to send his kid to such a school and that it will never = the School for 1. As before, when walking, I am conversing with the invisible so long as I am careful never to move my lips.

When we get to the athletic building, I climb to the second floor, bare assed. I have left clothes at Rice Jungle and am looking for a towel to wear on my way to find what is appropriate; by that I mean, "the garmet of eternity."

Plein air, within a larger group, someone trys to hang Unhelpful's bulky instrument like a millstone around my neck. Before they can I have handed the camera right back to them …

Quality Time Before the War

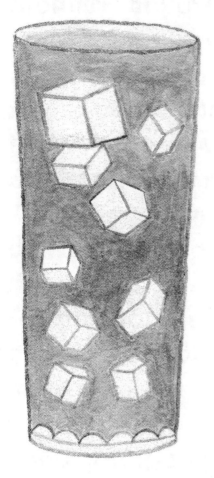 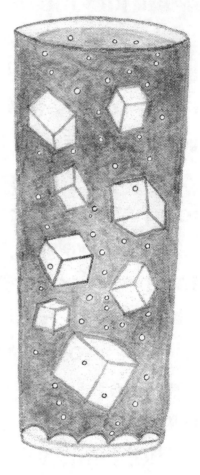

Unmixing the distant memory locus, 5915 Hermes Crescent, puts me way back where I never will belong, in Construe...where tonight the mysterious spotlight falls upon a scratched, skuffed walnut magazine rack between father's bed and the door of the bathroom...Behind that rack you might peer down through a narrow lead casement into a pleasant backyard with its sunny corner rose garden…adjacent the wind-flipped lily pads of a goldfish pond …

Besides an obsolete phone book, the magazine rack contains various expressions of 1950s photojournalism: *Saturday Evening Post, Look*, and the older, b&w version of *Life* magazine…Never much of a reader except for law, my father might thumb through one of these, yawning, before sleep.

I myself recollect a b&w cover portrait, below the red and white logo, of Sophia Loren, stunning in black V-neck. Age about nine or ten, I remember staring at it--even through it--transfixed & enraptured, not least by her almond eyes.

In the present episode, suspended, as it were, in air, superimposed before the magazine rack, I behold two highball glasses, two whiskeys I have mixed with ice and water, less often with ice and soda water, according to instruction.

Sometime in ancient spring, when my siblings were still away at boarding schools, the 3 of us must have been sitting out in that pleasant backyard in heavy metal lawn chairs. The air neither warm nor cool…Though he was not a continuously irascible type, my father seems to be scraping flecks of earwax, real or imagined, from his inner ear with the dull end of a nail file he always carries in his jacket pocket…If they were tired at the end of a long dull day, and didn't feel like getting up to mix their own, I might be impressed into service and sent to the bar to prepare 2 whiskeys.

Once, I recollect mixing his drink, as specified, a jigger and a half of aromatic Scotch over ice, "and not too much water." I carry both drinks carefully, liquid columns swaying, back out to the spring yard. I am surprised to be told that, in this case, I have got it wrong. After a single sip, he turns up his nose and flicks an additional spec off the nail file before imparting a mysterious verdict.

So I'll always remember, he tells me, "You think, if you get it wrong, just this once, you'll never have to again."

Baffled then and baffled today, I maybe have to stop asking what he might have intended, assuming that he intended anything. Never have to fetch another whiskey? He didn't say his drink was weak or too strong; too much ice? Though our exchange may have been for her benefit, to her it could not have been of less interest.

Her drink must be satisfactory. She seems thoroughly immersed in the garden section of the paper. The indifference may be feigned. It could be she senses--dimly--that I am old enough now to become acquainted with the notion that some days are bound to be rockier than others. Such an impression might serve the way a trip to the doctor serves, wherein the feared inoculation is preceded by a whiff of alcohol.

Once only and in brief--"please spare us the details"--I was introduced to my father's boss, the CDR. If he had a Christian name I was not made familiar with it. Whether his title derived from military service or from his riverfront yachting activities, I never learned. Later I found out he was among the first to pioneer the concept of zero tolerance. Then I knew only that he was the CDR of father's firm, very respectable in that distant day though it was dissolved decades ago, like father's prep school and the junior college attended by my mother.

There is usually one day in the life of every student when he is released from academic pursuit to visit a scene of real life gainful employment; i.e., the parental job site. On the day when I visited his firm I was granted a brief audience with the CDR. I don't remember much about the office; his own was larger than the others. I guessed that he was like the school principal in respect to teachers, though he seemed brisker than the school principal.

Time was permitted for a firm handshake and a brief joke. Events were moving on. I had no idea why. Though I now know it was not a whodunit, I am able to recall "the mystery brought home from the office" only generally. When I try to recall the CDR's face, all I can think of is a charcoal drawing by Edward Hopper, *Office at Night*, preliminary--presumably though not necessarily--to his oil of the same title. In the familiar sketch two figures in an office are glimpsed from an old elevated train, or "el," at night. The CDR, I think, looked like the gray, thin man of business seated behind the office desk in the Hopper drawing. In that drawing he is accompanied by his secretary, apparently a recent college graduate, who stands daughter like and resentfully attentive at a filing cabinet. In Hopper's oil painting of the same scene, the figures are radically altered. The male figure behind the desk has become younger; his gray hair has waxed yellow. His secretary, still attentive at the filing cabinet, also has changed, is no longer daughter like and collegiate, but has thickened to voluptuousness, becoming almost blowsy, almost in need of a girdle.

After my brief intoduction to the CDR, there were no further activities scheduled before noon, so I was allowed to wander about the firm which seemed intently busy. Occasionally a phone jangled. I heard father taking a call in his office.

As I meandered past the law library I glimpsed the junior partner at a long dully polished table. Without noticing me he busily parsed a red-spined volume from a mustard-colored stack at his elbow. I watched him making notes on one side of a yellow legal tablet he flipped overleaf.

In father's office the phone was still

occupied while I mused dreamily beside his desk, staring down from an office window at toy cars and ant like pedestrians stories below. In that distant era before universal air conditioning, the window was open a few inches and I could hear traffic honks and fall buses grinding distantly. Like my school home room, the window had a glass partition slanted in front of the sill to deflect drafts.

I wandered out to the reception area where Mrs. M, the firm's sharp elderly secretary, with suit jacket removed, was busy collating stacks of mimeographed paper at a desk. Briefly, eye-fully, she handed me a legal tablet to scribble on with a few Mongol pencils, the familiar kind father brought home, with its eraser crimped round in red copper. Without thought I began to designate two opposing fleets of space ships--one with swept-back fins, the other with stub fins with pod fuel tanks. Mrs. M commenced stapling together duplicate depositions with a firm punching movement involving her elbow and palm…By the time the slow differentiation of my galactic armadas had emerged, I was beginning to feel the need of red crayon for rocket exhausts and explosions as the opposed fleets began to decimate one another. (Without exception, the space comics in my room at home specified this was what they must do.)

At this forlorn instant an untoward event occurred. I have to specify "occurred" because--although I was the sole instigator and perpetrator--I did not feel present in the event…However dubious "temporary insanity" might sound, I really hadn't any notion what possessed me. I could argue there was a precedent in the case of my older brother who one Sunday after church informed both parents that he had swallowed his penknife and felt ill. His gesture effectively monopolized parental attention for the entire afternoon. Back then, in the Freudian '50s, Mother was so upset she was barely able to pilot the station wagon. The three of them sped to the hospital for x-rays which revealed…precisely nothing. My brother had made it all up …

My fleets were primed, ready to commence firing…With red crayon absent, I glanced from the yellow tablet toward Mrs M who frowned slightly, turning between stacks of collated stapled and collated unstapled documents, even as she continued to punch out with complete regularity.

Before I knew it, I had slipped off the smooth chair to jab my index finger into the stapler at the precise moment Mrs. M punched down on it. A needle of wire pierced the mashed tip of my finger in front of the nail. Blood began to drip.

It hurt me but it was poor Mrs M who cried out. What had she done! Precisely nothing… But then, how might events be construed? For an older woman not that close to retirement, the incident might well have seemed perilous. Though flustered, she was quick to supply a tissue for a blotch redder than the missing crayon…Almost instantly, it seemed, the junior partner from the library, who had heard her cry, was crouched beside me with a pair of tweezers from the office first aid kit. Realizing only that I had somehow tattooed myself, I stared dumbfounded as he dexterously unfastened and extracted the offending staple.

While all this was going on, I was overhearing dialogue between my father and the CDR through an opened door down the hall. Plainly, I had failed to involve either of them in my drama. I couldn't make out the matter of their discussion and wasn't old enough to understand it if I could. The music was easier. The CDR presided; my father supplied interjections which, though subordinate, were not lacking in clarity.

A few years further on, at our dinner table, I remember how he impressed my brother and me with the crucial nature of the wording of the firm's various document, depositions, and contracts. A slipped phrase, an article gone awry, could cost millions and, for my father, implied peril like the approach of death itself. Whenever he needed to the CDR had a way of communicating disapproval so my father felt it. The CDR's method involved silence more than bombast. There could not have been many slip-ups. But on occasion, when he got some detail dead wrong, father came home more than tired and we all felt it. From a distance the CDR's presence informed us of 1 thing. His intention of staying in business.

Out in the spring yard father scrapes somewhat feverishly, delicately anxious to be rid of the brown wax that plagues him. Not a healthy habit. Perhaps she will chid him a little, though she doesn't. If he is about to tell her more than she wants to know re zero tolerance and the CDR's displeasure, he knows in advance she will only become more deeply immersed in the garden section. Not her department. Some things are better left at the office; i.e., little pictures have big ears. Whereas inoculations may be of benefit, infection is of none. No one is going to question that she labored to bring 4 goldfish into the world, or that she held down a paying job not once during her lifetime. I am permitted to think that our yard, our house, the flipping goldfish pond, et al, have more to do with the CDR and my father than with her and her parents. It will take me years to realize that this was never the case. There could have been an idea that such misplaced identification would prove a mental asset to me in future, or, if I have gotten it wrong, there may have been no thought behind it at all.

He gets about as far trying to expand her sympathy for "our" struggle to please the CDR as I do trying to get him to approve one of the overly neat, elaborately diagrammed space ships I spent hours--with ruler and dip pen--inking onto strips of shelf paper. When it becomes a question of the evening newspaper versus one of my futuristic designs, newsprint is the hands-down victor:

"Get away!" he explodes, just once, and the lesson is learned.

Once and once only, in the company of 2 junior partners from the firm, we visit the old, yet-to-be-torn-down civic ball park with its rubbery hot dogs and wooden bleachers.

A little after noon, raincoat over left arm, checking his wristwatch, he emerges from the corridor after his conference with the CDR. Mrs. M provides a trembly explanation of my gauze-wound fingertip. The self-inflicted wound provokes his quizzical look. Kids do the darnedest things. More to the point; we are to meet mother at the TC Club for lunch. Events are moving on and we are running a bit late …

I become enamored of kites. Diamond kites, French war kites, and, stablest of all, the box kite. On Saturday afternoon I request that he take me and my newly assembled, blue and yellow box kite to the Jr. School athletic field. Lately, she has been reading aloud to me, in a vocabulary a little in advance of my own, re Wilbur and Orville.

"I'm tired," he states flatly.

There is to be a party that night at the golf club, one she figures they must attend. Among other notables, the CDR and his bride will be present. He doesn't want to but will go if permitted an afternoon nap. He has gotten to that stage, she realizes. So it falls to her to drive me.

The school's athletic field, unlike nearby parks and more public areas of the city, is deserted on Saturday morning. No scheduled activities. This is the pre Salk era and there is a real concern about crowds and polio.

Behind the yellow brick gym a hound sprints along the distant chain link fence that borders the field…Getting out of the car, I observe treetops grazed by the breeze …

As most kite aficionados could explain, the best launch supposedly involve 2 individuals.

One holds the kite lightly over their head while the flyer unrolls a few dozen yards of twine. At  a shout the holder releases the kite with an upward flick and the flyer runs forward into the wind. At her age, in Construe, in the 1950s, my mother is not about to cause a commotion stumbling around the Jr. School athletic field in high heels. So it's up to me. She will stay in the car parked on a side street beneath o'er spreading horse-chestnut trees. As she witnesses my assay through the first ever wraparound windshield, Metropolitan Opera (Tannhauser) muted on car radio, she maybe sighs thinking that in a few years, like my siblings, I will be away at school. Then it will be up to teachers and coaches and peers. Or, perhaps, this is simply a good moment for her to kick off her heels and relax, involving no thought at all.

Her Fleas

Two women. The one I'm with has no visual component but I can feel her presence. I'm physically near her, only a foot away…Further away I sight Molested-in-Puberty (not by me!) from the B Ave. commune, TM 7. I used to wonder if her sexual abuse, by a relative, was an act of class possession.

She approaches me, eternally in her twenties, uninvested, nubile. Her problem is she now has fleas she wants to be rid of, or rather, she wants me to rid her of them. She has the thought I might be of some use, but I'm recalcitrant as I explain, "You must get rid of them yourself." However, before I tell her I show her some things she will want to make choices about. These are objects with a physical, geometric presence, though as to what their functions might be--if they have functions--no hint is given.

One of the objects is like the transparent

plastic box at the market used to package strawberries. Tiny "hairs" grow out of the berries, resembling "fleas." The plexi container has buttons on its corner that snap shut. All I can do to help rid her of fleas is preselect the shapes she will want to make choices about.

Upath

A place like my cousin's at Ink Lake, make that Tea Leaf Lake, though it's not my cousin's. A little girl, a child 3-4 years old, has been for her lesson to

adjust "blank check empathy." The parents who earlier parked her have returned to pick her up...She smiles at her teacher before departing. The teacher, on my left, has no visible component. Is there any better way to describe the subject being taught? The girl is being tutored or given lessons.

Before she departs, she smiles at her teacher. Her smile moves me; I feel in my heart area that she loves her teacher. Now when she smiles, she shows her teeth, depicted the way cartoonists sometimes depict a woman's teeth as a single white piece. Despite the convention, I feel she loves her teacher.

Cut to Xmas casual…How well I recollect those times standing in line, eyes closed 6:15AM outside the main post office, Nivon City; Xmas casual line up, downtown, about one thousand again this year for 3 wk's temp work. High school kids, old wine bibbers, rubbies, ashen East Indian women with overcoats worn over saris. I could almost sleep on my feet. Dawn reddens behind buildings. Not until 8AM does the line sludge around the corner…In the meantime, for a morale booster, a mobile home equipped with a tinny loudspeaker is brought forward to rasp "White Christmas," transcribed how many decades ago by that Pepsodent chorus …

Soon though, I am returned to the U.S.S.R. with my 4-star generalized sister. In a car someone else drives there is no familiar voice and no other voice. I don't know who or what principle is behind the wheel, which is like the teacher who cannot be visualized or rendered transparent. Sister is in the front right seat; I am in the back right seat. Across the border in "Russia," as we are driven through a landscape, I play a game with her. The idea is…some games are worth playing. Others could even be harmful. We have been playing one car game; now we are playing another. The game we are playing involves gazing out vehicular windows at landmarks, aspects of landscape we are passing. An unfamiliar landscape may or may not contain boulders. The game is considered worth playing because it is psychic. So far, all I know is it involves studying landscape with the idea that my sister, by telepathy or a 6th sense, could know every thought as I am thinking it. Of course, she would not. I have not, as yet, figured out a science experiment that could prove or explode any such theory.

Pictures from Bean Town

I leaf through a book of old photographs and texts. It's like a centennial picture book, this time not about Construe but re Bean Town with an article or two concerning zeppelin races …

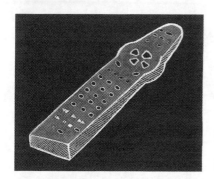

I see a short man who is big and fat with thick teeth. He looks like AG, that chubby Jewish kid in my grammar school except this time he is English, also, with thick lips and a small pointed head like a Gogol caricature. He carrys a pool cue and tells me he is headed toward Varsity Cinemateque. The hall where he is going to shoot pool, everybody knows, is directly across from Cinemateque.

In E. Dickenson's Bean Town, I kiss a woman on her cheek near her temple. I feel flesh yield beneath my lips. Beneath her flesh I sense her body's firmness, her bones.

Hardly statuesque, she wears a slim dress, hair rather short. After I kiss her she says the timing was good because she is about to phone her employer and the kiss will render her confident in conversation with her boss. I imagine her on an old black phone dialing her employer and at the same time phoning alumni. Does she still work for them? Among others, Cassius Clay has noted the importance of knowing who you work for.

(See "Contract.")

In Bean Town I cast my gaze across the river toward a large aluminium dome in which our play is to be reenacted. I want to take a bus over there to see the play, but until the tour group understands that our cook, E, was never a daughter of Compulsion's Plum, I won't have carfare.

Also, there are worm-shaped larvae I don't eat …

Conference of 1

Burgeoning pop explosion!…cartoons, loony tunes, sugary sodas, laughtrack sitcom mind candy; 1930s (VCR) "screwball comedies" midst crackerjack glitz bits…et, cetera…as if an electrode had probed the very brain node / memory center that releases it all in advance …

Walking west with Irascible on my left, I realize he is about to send Uses Milk up into the antique hotel to cut a deal with Beloved Entertainer who is up there, supposedly, and has written (or has had written) his Bio "as told to." He wants her to negotiate a juicy contract, but I argue B.E. is never going to relish one of her ilk, being already so overfamiliar with it.

Instead the book discussion group meets to discuss B.E.'s schlock Bio. At an oval table a man and his wife are seated behind me. He yaks on and on, interlarding his talk with anecdotes artfully selected from the negotiable Bio.

Meantime, in the background, his bride vamps continuously on harmonica. Cut to…the Praries, highly conventionalized 1930s images…Grain that was sewn in town parks and vacant lots… wherever there was any room…is now being harvested by a crew of hobos and "depression era" itinerants garbed in rags. One with upturned collar and pulled down hat has escaped from a Max Ernst collage. The harvest is part of a gov't project I witness in a park near a road. The harvesters' sickles incorporate pen knives. As they swipe, muted Sonny Terry harmonica cuts a jivey rhythm in the background…It's understood that the harvest will continue "until I be signed to the signature of death no longer."

Sharpness. Bottle of ink & dip pen. I think of tedious one and a half page themes I copied out in elementary school. Unhelpful tension accidentally smacked the bottle of ink, overturning a black spill across the theme page it had taken me an hour to copy…At the time I remember mentioning something to Mother about a "contract" …

At just this point Unhelpful presses upon me several negatives with the white hair weirdly retouched. I hand them immediately back to him, just like the camera. Next he wants a $1000 loaner for a round trip to the old country…He starts out loudly interdicting me before he falls immediately silent.

So I must…pull myself up and over the chin-up bar to flip down inside a conference room which resembles the refurbished waiting room of an Amtrack station. I sit with others around an oval conference table…Just like Ye Olde Dreamwerke Shoppe…A man who is standing is supposedly a politically important scribe, though the importance is ironic so long as we assume that it is…An older seated man asks the standing one a question which requires particular knowledge. The standing one does not recall what he has been programmed to recall; he knows his stuff, all right, but seems unwilling to force memory; this amounts to a temporary failure of imagination on the part of the examiner…During the oral exam, fellow members of the conference, to my left and right, have clamped their hands firm as duct tape across my mouth. I forcibly peel away their paws so I can speak, though I am not forced to speak.

This places me where I have been. At the top of a cliff overlooking a beach. No news isn't good news, but all news = non sequitor. This time there is chain-link fence at the cliff's edge. I fling sand I have scooped up over the fence and watch it float down in a cloud into the water below. It makes a pleasant shhhhh-shhhhh sound as it hits still water. Then I turn to a black-haired woman in a white dress standing nearby. She is rather thin, her cheeks pinched. Crouched before her, I reach up to grasp her right thigh. I notice that her ankle is thin and that she is a bit knock-kneed like

Ms. M. I think of expressing many things to her, for once, instead of Uses Milk. Somehow I get the idea she would be receptive, just as formerly I could only have assumed that Uses Milk would be. "Hold me," she resumes, although I have maintained my unremitting clasp on her thigh.

Newsprint

Although we have not leisure to form a clear interpretation of the last, we are being dragged on to the next by a gov't spotlight which has shifted. (Been shifted.)

Due to the intervention of an egregious superego, I know I must try to avoid political thinking whenever that is possible.

2.

The streets in town are muddy.

Presently the vehicle is a trolley car/boat that I seem to have boarded with a group of politicized youth. Splashing ocher waves right and left, we churn toward the newsprint building.

Outside walking near a building, where Unhelpful Bro used to rent, at first there appear to be no windows. Then I see a young woman dressed in white with white cloth-covered buttons on her jacket. Her clothes are smudged with something like silt. As I enter the lobby, I briefly encounter Unhelpful before it is reported that a woman has been shot dead by a 2nd woman.

The murderer is the young brunette with a (not 2) shortcut. The murderer lifts her own nightie, pointing out horrible scratch marks and lacerations which the dead woman inflicted on her up to--but not including--her breasts, down her torso and the sides of her legs, to her feet. It occurs to me that the dead woman must have had very long fingernails.

We start to scale the facade of the newsprint building. When we are fairly high up, the thick heavy white paper which covers its exterior--except for windows and window ledges that we explore for hand and footholds--starts to separate from the building …

3.

Almost before I know it, I am aboard a C-119. The empty cargo section is cube-shaped and has a lower level like an aluminium pan to soak a paint roller...Someone hands me a 7 foot wingspan...The idea is I am supposed to jump from the vehicle, with the 7 foot wing held across my middle, and spiral down thousands of feet to the ground, which I see moving past below out the open cargo bay. I think that the wing is not supportive enough and am wary of jumping...Whoever handed me the wingspan displays a sideview diagram of an airfoil to persuade me there will be enough lift.

Again the vehicle changes...this time into a 2-wheeled electrocycle I ride up a steep hill... Near the top, the road is torn. The asphalt stripped to reveal a salt flat beneath. A foot or so below asphalt I follow my path on a bumpy ride and am transported further uphill to dismount at a flower market. Sprayers are releasing atomized water mist that drifts over and around the market. A news stand forms part of the market.

Various papers from different cities are laid out on a table. In one one of these, returned to Chinatown, I plod into a newsprint office to collect the most recent edition. They hand me a copy of a Peking daily, half page aquatint, page 1. I notice that the newspaper office doubles as a restaurant. Meats and other foods are kept without refrigeration on a big shelf over the door. Four restaurant workers take down the food to inspect it. They do not look healthy. Three are Chinese, one is Caucasian. One has his face bandaged in gauze.

Next summer, iron bowl in hand, having returned to Rice Jungle, I notice that a stack of old newspapers next to the wood stove is strangely un-yellowed. I start to examine one edition, thinking it is probably early 1970s time period and that the lead article + front page photo will surely concern Dick Nixon. On closer inspection the date is '81 and has nothing to do with Tricky Dick. The photograph shows an inner city Negro and concerns the U.S. economy.

On the road between Middle School and Senior School, I encounter a man reading a newspaper. Time period 1950s. I want to tell the average reader good news about JFK but first I try to examine his copy for the exact date. The date is printed in a foreign language in an alphabet unknown to me though not, I would assume, to Foreign Language Student …

In a vague dorm on a vaguer campus I have neglected my studies, have not attended the single lecture, have even forgotten the subject. A brass heirloom that gives the date and time is on my bedspread, then on the dresser. I would repair to the lecture hall to see if I might catch up before the final. A student passing out mimeographs for her professor hands me quite a stack, printed on Bristol board. I sit down to check the pages…A gray animal with bristly hair jumps over my head and flys like a scurrying shot to the head of the class where it ricochets off the blackboard back toward… me me me me me…Like a paperclip sped from a rubber band, the instant I begin to prepare the exam, I have passed it and graduated.

Resembling an overly familiar rosary bead, the cliched cultural eidetic circles past again… After a tough day, Dad's head is slumped behind newsprint. Son approaches with drawing to show him, inked on a strip of shelf paper. It is a 1950s conception of a three-stage rocketship, copied industriously from a drug store scifi magazine. Does Mother form the prime audience, on a sofa in the background, or has she exited, already weary of this round before it begins? Aware he is tired, do I by any chance, expect I can annoy him into anger in order to seem more noble in her eyes? I think not. Anyway, he makes it clear his interest lies in newsprint, not my drawing.

Turning the pages for some real news, I note an ad for "reel-to-reel," but can't think of any reason to buy it.

Instead, I hang onto the side of a steep mountain with one hand…and to the fist of a child, a boy of around seven or eight, with the other. According to Elizabeth Bishop, the danger lies in falling down. I assume she must be part right. However, below me, I see a road cut into the mountainside and consider how I might reach it. When I turn to the left, the child has disappeared (again)…I crawl toward a cave with bricks in a semicircular frame layered around the entrance. Inside a man is protected from Chinese snow falling outside the cave entrance.

Ten thousand years late, I visit a nuclear dump which has come to resemble an ordinary landfill. Trash metal has been tossed from a cliff higher up onto the heap here below.

There is a woman in the cave as I leave it. The room adjacent contains patients in beds and several machines that give an electroshock when touched. One of the machines has tiny white ceramic sockets for flashlight bulbs. Most of the sockets are empty with the exception of a single bulb which glows dimly. The last machine produces an additional shock which angers me; I write out some anger for the patients.

The following summer at Rice Jungle, while fishing from my cousin's raft, I snag a sheet of newsprint from a stack on the bottom. It is strangely colored and printed and I'm showing it to another person…Around the paper's edge, enveloped in the frame, are two combs, one with teeth far apart, both clear plastic…(Outside of a sod hut, a news sheet on the desert floor headlines "an ancient Cretan" or "stupid person.")

I follow a group of children, a kindegarten. On an urban street we toddle downstairs into the blank classroom. Each child carrys an individual scrap of newsprint, blank except for a comb glued to the margin with rubber cement. The teacher is a nice firm lady resembling Mrs. Albright, so perhaps this is the School for 1.

Each is to write his exam on his own page; if you pass, the prize is the comb which is then peeled away from the margin…I am receiving instructions from the teacher seated at her desk. Because of thought, I have immediately passed the exam, so the comb is detached from my page…Now the other children are in an adjacent room. Without words teacher indicates that a comb is not necessarily the prize, that I should determine what the prize is myself…I misplace a loaf of raisin bread…Real raisin bread, not processed white bread with raisins inserted for credibility…A firm solid loaf of raisin bread = to the immensity of space …

For now, though, I must run fast like the skinny old dude I see jogging toward the aquatic center. Inside, are two swimming pools. I'm not clear on what takes place in the first. Lessons? I move to my right. Someone has tossed a cat into the water, which is silt gray in color…I need to move my bowels. I go to the bathroom where I sit on the toilet glancing at a copy of the community paper printed on shiny, coated stock like an old student newspaper. Nostalgiawise, I recollect praise I got for an article on the trustees' meeting, written to Headmaster's exacting specifications. Despite the paper's shiny texture, I use one page to clean my anus. The *puer aeturnus* is seated on the commode to my right. I crap a long thin stool in a spiral, emptying my bowels…A few people stand around, smiling self-contemptuously. They seem to look to me, as if I were to tell them something. I tell them clear out since they don't need to use the facilities. It surprises me no end when they clear out.

Now I can swim the long tunnel through rock. My lungs are about to explode when I surface inside a cave of clear blue water. The surface is completely still and, mysteriously, reflects the sky …

What has been up to now a preview for a movie featuring the only well-known 1950s crooner, is situated in a clean, not particularly neat kitchen at night. A musician friend of the crooner is supposed to be some kind of addict and is seated at the formica table. A piece of clean newsprint is spread before him on the table. Beside it a double jar contains liquid being filtered through a square of newspaper inserted between the two jars. The musician is holding a big empty hypodermic he twirls around his finger like a six-shooter. He doesn't use the syringe.

In the bathroom there is no toilet and no stove. However, the wall toward the airshaft is warm. In fact as I look I see that the plaster has cracked and that there is a hole punched through ribs of lath. We look through the hole down into a large high-ceiling'd room that previously did not exist. The floor is brown lino with newspaper spread over a section of floor out from the wall. Articles...of furniture have been placed on top of newspaper. I notice also a hole punched in the wall of this other room which has let in snow and moisture so the room is slightly damp. (Newspaper is being used to absorb moisture.) Immediately below there is a door arc'd partway open and draped over the top of it, neatly folded, a green plaid blanket and, beneath the blanket, some garments.

The youth on my right takes a flat brass curtain runner, curved at one end, and reaches down to fish the blanket and garments off the top of the door. Once he has retrieved them he climbs down into the high-ceiling'd room up onto a stage where he begins crooning into an old-fashioned mic. I am able to see through to his anima which resembles a girl who belonged to the anti-nuke group that used to meet at a derelict WWII hanger...When I see that his anima resembles her, he quits singing right after crying outloud, "I am really hurting."

Examining the TV screen closer to, I observe the image in black and white, a pastel drawing of a courtroom drama...Seated is a molasses-hued Negress, exceedingly thin, about fifty.

The only motions in court, the rolling of her eyes to accompany the drumming of her fingers. She, also, appears to have lost patience with the proceedings, even though such may not be her case.

Exhibit A: how could I forget the smooth, cold pipe rail fence--bent from fat kids--that we had to sit on in front of Junior School while awaiting a late car pool? Where is she? So late--with nostalgia absent--that I must go live in a world under the ground where the task is…crumple sheets of paper …

Also, I should bathe outside in the public fountain of the hotel before strolling back through the lobby in a hotel bathrobe toward my healthiest cell. Passing the lobby news-stand, I consider risking a few coins before I notice copies people have already abandoned on a bench along the wall. I examine the date when she approaches. Ordinary-colored hair. I'm not too clear on her intentions but one thing she does is cover my mouth with her hand. This causes a freight elevator to open on both sides. I look through to the other side where a worker is loading garbage to send down. He begins to wax expansive regarding his homespun philosophy. I shouldn't stray to listen but walk on down the corridor toward a display case where I check out today's tabloid; cover photo of an editor shaking her fist in a contrived gesture.

Walk on, walk on kiosk overplastered with multi notices, toward another paper, stained with diluted blood, describing war in Middle East, as a jeep rolls in off the desert with "news for friends."

I arrive back at 3818, only it's not my room; I'm in B's, across the hall. Seems I have been out riding an electrocycle around and around in circles...When I enter the Chinatown bank, the withdrawl slip is ancient newsprint and the air-cooled bank...deserted...Back in B's room I keep trying to clear phlegm from my t'roat so I can speak to the person in the room down the hall; who that person may be isn't so transparent. I walk out to spit phlegm into a common toilet.

In a tiny room which used to belong to Inaudible Knock, papers from different cities are strewn across the bed. Also, a thick paperback with a red & white cover, *Soft Fire.* I approach childhood's dresser. Above it, glued to my wall like a picture frame, is a thin, unopened cardboard box. Through the celophane window I see that box contains lead soldiers, still tabbed to the back.

Different room, same house. I sit at a wooden table with some water colors. Placed on top

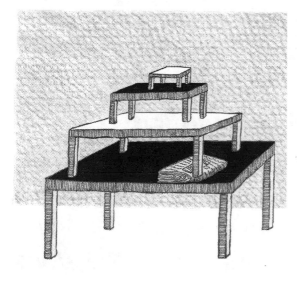

of the wooden table is a 2nd, wobbly card table with legs unfolded. One of the legs rests on folded newspaper with red watercolor brushed along the fold.

During the cultural revolution an individual tattooed "politically incorrect" by *our* committee would sometimes be re-educated by being forced to construct a pagoda of such tables, one upon another, higher and higher, until it collapsed, spilling the tainted bureaucrat down hard. Bones were broken and skulls cracked. And yet, it was always time to begin afresh, until the retrainee was too damaged to continue.

Therefore I have happened to become an independant, private operative in this town, your town, who, when he reads a notice in gazette or tribune, a notice advertising "free country weekend," decides he will test drive almost any brand of human potential therapy with "fee to follow full registry." Should the operative require a spring-wound plot, TV shows...location of the group's ashram on tidal cove. Cove is polluted now because of a mud bottom but whenever the clip is shown filters click into place to emphasize *the sky's reflection.* (Not unlike--should goback4?--an earlier cave.)

I am said operative visiting the ashram. Inside, I aggressively introduce myself to the therapists, all men, and remove the newspaper notice alongside a half sheet of copy paper from my pocket. I consult the therapists stagily and ironically as though playing to an invisible audience. I want the invisible to know that I don't take the rhetoric of therapy too seriously. I sit down in an armchair which becomes a piano stool and begin "playing piano"; that is, kidding the therapists who seem not at all rebuffed but laugh, as though going along with a dumb joke. They have not told me their names so I dub one of them "Ralf," saying, "It's always Ralf, isn't it," laughing ironically as I slap him across the knee. He laughs, agreeing his name is Ralf.

Noon.

To hop on one foot before another = Chinese cerimonial dance. I proceed to perform hara-kiri;

stabbing myself in the lower right abdomen with a silver dagger; however, the knife blade sticks out of white birch. There is no pain so it must be illusion; i.e., I see the blade itself cut at an angle near the handle so as to appear stabbed into the abdomen when held against it.

Cut to C St. Her house looks different now, more vertical. I walk along one side of it in the company of another. It is future time, all external structures decimated. There is a woman in the house--not a mother--for whose health and welfare I am responsible...The other and I look down the drive to C Street where I see a huge cylinder of paper I think must have fallen off a truck. At first I think it's probably a big roll of newsprint like the ones the Immigrant Word Engineer and I discovered dumped, yellowed, and overgrown with brambles on our hike to the bottom of a ravine on the edge of St. John's Harbour, Newfoundland, on a summer car trip decades ago...I am not clear that it is actual newsprint despite the size of the roll...I trust it's not bumwad although a steel fixture or spindle seems to be a part of it …

In the aerodrome I gaze from the picture window at the zeppelin coming in for a landing at an extreme angle…Suddenly…vehicle drops like a shot and has crashed on its nose… Outside I stand behind a barricade examining the wreckage. In front on the right a couple of sniggerers begin to chortle.

Later, back aboard the zepp, I am enjoying a slow, gentle flight over a landscape of rolling hills until I am distracted when something tumbles outback…graft trees in cylindrical containers.

"Parents slid out the mind of."

The zepp makes a forced landing; I must goback4 graft trees before proceeding...

Returned to the mother ship, I encounter a voluptuous young woman who stands directly in front of me. "It's all right," she says. "You

give them to me." When them = rolls of paper I see tumble into a plastic sack she opens …

Just before, while outside the vehicle retrieving those plants, I notice pink lightning flash behind clouds. Although I was never led to believe a thunderstorm should follow an airship, someone has the impression that the zeppelin was not designed for extreme weather and must, therefore, strive continuously to stay just ahead of, or just behind, *der sturm.*

without (within) any vehicle
or any instrument of flight

Driving my father's old sedan, I am surprised by a mountain added at the entrance to the 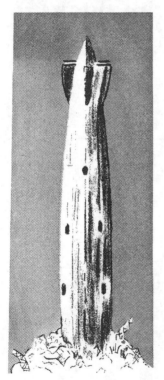 bay. "Sort of like Gibraltar," I surmise as I drive up a mountain road to a residential area where I get out of the car. Although it's supposed to be an affluent section, the only dwellings are dilapidated shacks where a drunkard, that 1940s novelist must have lived...mortared, creosoted logs...walkways over tidal mud...An unclarified woman is on my left...With her and a group I look out from the mountain into vast clear sunny air.

An absolutely brand spanking new zeppelin is approaching the mountain despite terrific winds buffeting it to the right and left. It has to tack back and forth like a sailboat. There is a toylike quality to it ("The Sunday Zeppelin" by Saroyan) but it's full size and carrys passengers…The zeppelin turns past the mountain and settles down at the gas station at 4th & H to refuel. On the ground it is no bigger than a car. In the air it is both tiny and enormous; its size is missing…When it takes off after refueling, it tears on some tree branches adjacent to the garage and explodes in billowing hydrogen flames.

I drive father's car back down the mountain, down along the shore, to find myself in a different city, where I rent a cabin in a motor court and lie on 1 side in bed looking out 1 window at a startlingly clear cold sunny day, people, wind, sky, buildings in brilliant sunshine.

Next time up in the air, I am adrift in an undirected, free balloon. In the wicker basket with me is a woman who surrounds me like a small room. There is no visual perception but I have a sense of her surrounding me like the near walls of the small room from previous episodes.

I think Inferior Commitment will always find his room too small. Interior Commitment is another matter.

The balloon's flight is over the costal city on a sunny day, a little like yesterday…Everything is clear and distinct as I look down at the city below. I can pick out buildings and the harbor or--if it happens to be rivers--where they meet, also boats a few thousand feet below.

Abruptly, there is no view; the woman surrounding me has vanished. Without a bump, I'm on the ground across from Metropolis. I have an awareness = to the absence of transition. I say outloud, to myself in particular, "What sense does this make? I'm soaring in a balloon; suddenly, the balloon disappears."

In an enclosure, a booth again, of stone this time, I look back across shallow water toward the skyline. The booth has an opening a couple of feet wide at one end. The episode has color but it's not drunkard's technicolor;

instead, everything is textural. I experience texture by looking at the buildings. I look back across water at separated buildings.

Three men approach; I know them to be police although they are not in uniform. Inside the enclosure, the walls are close. The police stand in front of me, smiling weirdly. I ask them, "Have I broken the law? Is there going to be conflict of interest? If so, please inform me, what the most beneficial conflict might be." They make no mention of Xpendables but continue their approach, smiling eerily …

To catch my breath I sit, for a moment, at the edge of her pool with a flashlight that spins around rapidly before it flys outward from my hands. By thought I am able to direct its flight, but not completely; I observe that it has somewhat a will of its own. I watch the flashlight fly into the swimming pool only to churn through the water, now with a glass handle on it like a beer stein…When it emerges from the pool it is transformed into a long necked bottle…I warn a man standing near the bottle not to be transformed into a statue …

Next, I address a film director who has his bare feet pressed against my left and right abdomen. Gruffly, he informs me, success is hollow…Balls of chocolate spangled with beads of colored sugar roll into the girls' rooms…VG in black is on my left; she kisses me and says something flattering to steer me down toward the elevator. I squeeze the inside of her thigh because I don't want to go down.

Flying in a room I float in air as if it were water. Then, outside in the unfamiliar city, I fly over a roof. The sense is I can direct my flight, make it go the direction I want, though slowly. I land beside a chimney. I press forward into the chimney, into a single room. Inside, I confront several word dealers, vaguely familiar, seated at table. They smoke shreds in a pipe they offer me. Just now, don't feel like having any …

Brother, in a corridor room between rooms, sits down at the table to make a phonecall after handing me a pipe, chrome plated, which looks familiar. I ask if it is In(f)erior or In(t)erior Commitment's pipe. He reiterates: "No, I don't think so." I want to understand who the pipe actually belongs to; I know it's not anyone I remember or know already. The word I smoke in it is particularly good.

Returned from a voyage to Isolate Island, I must drive my electrocycle through cold, slushy streets. I'm not that familiar with the city but trailing behind me, attached to the electrocycle, is a train of small wagons, each packed with unknown cargo. I park the vehicle, dismount, and stumble through wet snow, trying to get my bearings. Where is the cargo transporting me; where am I transporting it and where am I going to spend the night? When I would return to the electrocycle, I have forgotten where I parked it.

Now I am pedaling a child's tin pedal car. My legs are exactly the right length to reach the pedals. The streets are snow-filled near the antique hotel where I am staying with Mother & Sister. I return to the hotel after parking the pedal car. In a square, dark-paneled room Mother & Sister engage in conversation which excludes me, or I have begun to think about something else. I understand I have forgotten where I parked the pedal car. I think ex pal, Miss World War I, must know where I parked it.

So I am returned to the vehicle. Returned to the very spot, I find it clarified to transparence again.

Abruptly, I am witness to a tidal wave, evoked by an earlier drawing, as it rolls across the ocean. Though large enough to destroy anything in its path, something alive, white--a flying fish, is it?--arcs o'er top the wave to land on the other side without being destroyed.

In a further scene near the costal city: the wave is visible from the beach as it rolls tumbling toward Metropolis...On the beach a gigantic wall like a waffle iron on its side is mounted on wheels. It is as big as several high-rise apartments joined together over numerous ore truck tires. I'm moving the vehicle as quickly as I can along the beach to shield Metropolis from the oncoming wave.

Suddenly I find myself inside wall/vehicle. Inside it's like a vast space ship which rumbles as it moves. There are many people running, hither and yon, along dusky corridors, helping to make preparations that will buffer the wave.

The interior is constructed of concrete to resemble an industrial building with squeeze buckets, mops, and piles of cardboard boxes lining the corridors. Kind of a mess, though at last there is room to move around.

Even so, can't help thinking of Piranesi's Max Security which I visited several years back…Point of view then was looking out a bulletproof plate windshield moving through an armored, hexagonal tunnel...There were many intersections so the vehicle started and stopped often.

The prison consisted of those tunnels which, I remember, were lined with templates like a space platform. Individual cells weren't visible but perhaps the doors off corridors led to them...Voice-over explained that, of the prisoners, some had sentences "as long as 10,000 years." There was a musical sound track to the visit which resembled the sound track of a children's cartoon show featuring super-heros, heroines, and tin robots, interspersed with violence amid technical stunts.

Inside the present wall/vehicle are slit-like windows you look out. As the vehicle rumbles along I regard the passing street where I notice my electrocycle parked exactly where I left it. I consider climbing outside to ride off on the electrocycle though it feels stunting and wrong to abandon the large vehicle.

Driving father's old car, from which I earlier removed a camera, I line up behind other vehicles on a semicircular drive…Just ahead is the entrance to a building I want to go into because I don't know what building it is. Should be 21st Century Club in Construe? Or a dishwashing restaurant? Or could be an old dance class = to a tediously familiar rosary bead, shopworn eidetic relating Ms. AC and mi madre.

Go back 4what? 4$$? 4 the 1&only establishing shot? I have *paid* to tag along as mere assistant on this dig. Ergo, I refuse, contractually, to rescreen the identical same box of dirt, one more time, again, if that fails to turn up a single beneficial artifact.

I think maybe an attendant is going to emerge to take the car and park it so you can go in. However, there seems to be a holdup as we wait behind some vehicles, ahead of others, in the unmoving lineup. When I notice a doorman out front, I get out of the car to ask him regarding the consistency of the holdup. Why is it taking forever to get inside?

The moment *I* get out to speak to the doorman, my vehicle is stolen by police. What law has been broken? In a detail from an earlier effort, it was *the cop* who emerged, billy club in hand. Without asking, I know I'll have to pay $6 to get the car back. I start to approach the ones who impounded my vehicle but now they seem to flee into the little room. I pursue them into camera lucida, the little room, where the feeling is the same as in the cabin, booth, or lt hskpng under the stairs; i.e., walls closing in, squeezing me no matter where in the room I happen to stand… Curtains wrap around me; could they be the toy cape that kid in daycare wore to mime a superhero? Concentrated, not much space…

When I approach the police with money to get the car back, I notice that the left cheek of one of them, just below the eye, has been punctured and pierced by wires, or safety pins …

So I guess it must be through necessity that I invent this wing to ride air currents. I find it effective, small, flexible; turned at just a slight angle, it carries me up hundreds of feet over a landscape…What could be a 1950s women's dormitory drifts below. If I bend the wing to the right or left, just slightly, it moves in that direction. Descent to a damp grassy hillside is equally rapid …

With two others I enter a park along the shore. As on zeppelin day, it's windy. There is the usual drop off to the ocean below where familiar waves break over rocks seen before. I have a piece of cloth, which is disc-shaped, which I try out as a parasail. It carries me up twenty feet near the edge of the park. I am almost blown out over the ocean but manage to land back in the park…I recount my near disaster to others who have been exploring the park on their own.

We leave the park to proceed along the shore. The girders of the B or G Street Bridge are visible ahead and to the right, outlined black against blue morning sky...We continue on into a hospital. All chambers are not recalled at once, nor should they be. In one chamber several galvanized metal discs are found rotating in the floor, like turntables, in a car garage. Within the same room a chunk of dry

ice orbits elliptically, a comet smashing occasionally into metal walls, causing icy chunks to crash to the floor.

Outside my mother's hospital, looking back at the complex, one other is with me, seated beside me on the park bench. We await the other other, who remains within, who will join us.

A subsequent instrument of flight consists of a pole with a triangular attachment. Like a kid on a toy horse I run with it across a playing field and am carried sometimes to quite a height by the breeze; sometimes I manage to get only a few feet off the ground. Then, inside a large museum hotel, I hover outside partway opened elevator doors of a large freight elevator filling with children. Against a wall, perpendicular to the elevator, is a semicircular table. On it, a vinyl tripod case for the telescope tripod I was permitted to aquire decades ago during a childhood tour through Germany. I see that the tripod has been removed, trashed most likely by one of my brother's kids. Awaiting the other other, I am in no hurry, not in any degree anxious to zoom through elevator doors opened…partway …

Walking out an ocean dock, I carry a musket which is also a fishing pole with a chronometer mounted on it as well. The chronometer is like the odometer of the electrocycle. I see children fishing for rock cod and sunfish, as I did on Isolate Island. Looking over the right side of the dock, I see a big lobster crawl out onto some rocks. I climb down from the dock and approach the creature for a better look. The lobster turns into an armadillo which scurrys inland. The armadillo transforms into a sheep which I slaughter and butcher with the small pocket knife I thought worth keeping. First, I remove the fleece before portioning the meat …

Out back of the newspaper building, as though triumphant, I soar and spiral up to the roof…The roof is a cliff looking out over the ocean; waves break monotonously over ocean rocks seen below. The school is off to my left, a quarter mile away along the top of the cliff. I jump out from the cliff and soar upward, hoping to catch an air current that will carry me over yonder to the School for 1…I try to fly toward it though I am not in absolute control. Looking below I see, floating up toward me from the island, a changed vehicle.

Over a yellow-green vale, conscious of questions of speed and direction, I get no answer but manage to keep thinking.

And the following night, observe a shooting star as it streaks toward the horizon. At the point where it would burn up, the meteor turns into a flying saucer. I mention this amid the ex nihilo tour group. The saucer flys to different quadrants of the sky, tipping at different angles. Next, I am holding the plastic lid of an oatmeal container in both hands. It is "a saucer" and enables me to take off and fly to the four corners of the sky.

Instantly, my vehicle has become a square of cardboard. I hold onto it with both hands and am enabled, though there is some problem to do with flying I am not able to define, and I pray about it as I pass over a crowded street below, near a public beach, over a group of four young girls...Then somewhat higher, above a dry, dusty, late summer/early fall athletic field, I look down on the mild heat float; on a few children playing; and on the straw-colored lampshade I decorated for Ideas-per-Second...I fly toward a domed building at the edge of the field, chanting, in Latin, "Fee-days, feeeee-days," (faith) over and over. As I approach the dome, with ideas of alighting on its ledge, I hear my brother-in-law's mother mention something to me, although I can't quite make out her words.

I know a mystery or suspense film involves

the tour group. It's not so much that a criminal is being tracked down as that a mystery is being solved or dissolved. Ultra modern, lightweight pistol shoots a duplicate weapon out of another hand...Then I've found the culprit. A woman in her late forties, early fifties, with slight resemblance to my brother-in-law's mother. She tries to run but I tackle her on the lawn. She thrashes vigorously but I won't let go. I've caught her. For now.

I stand leaning one elbow on top of father's

bureau dresser back in Construe. When I turn to my left I observe him behind a desk in a narrow, one room study. In the course of our imaginary discussion he says, "Well now, how about that mystery brought home from the office?" I imagine a genre mystery on a bookshelf amid other volumes.

Also, I reflect on the day I made the drawing. My leg was in a cast after I had slipped and fallen from a cliff onto ocean rocks, an accident which could have cost me my life. Question is, whether the accident might also have terminated my redundancy. The way I felt making the drawing--on a slowed-down, sentient assembly line, to dissect the war economy--was that my experience itself was sufficient. It wasn't death: and was sufficient unto itself.

Hermes Crescent, the dining room. I observe the window next to the swing door into the pantry with curtains drawn. I hear voice-over pronounce an unfamiliar name: "Antisthenes." Outside the window, through cracks around the curtain, I see light from the driveway. I think it must be father's headlights, home late from the office. However, the light is not

headlights, but brighter and softer…a pale lunar light.

   Awake, and because it sounded like a real name, I look up the noun, "Antisthenes," to find there actually was such a person, founder of the Cynic school of philosophy…And I had never heard the name before or read a word about him …

On my left appears the unclarified woman who endeavors to turn me into a wolf…I look to the right and see the bedroom window with shades down. Again, the very bright cool lunar light appears in the space between the edge of the shade and the window frame. It moves across the top of the frame and down the right side. I think "flying saucer" and wake feeling *defended.*

Now a strataship has been assembled from squares of silvery metal. It contains a capsule that is about to be jettisoned. The other passenger aboard the capsule is a youth of about twenty. The question is whether or not the capsule will descend toward the surface of the planet. The youth seems to think it's going to ascend toward an orbital position where a clear view of the heavens will be possible. A button is pressed. I open my eyes to discover that I've neither descended to the surface, nor gone into orbit, and that the youth has vanished. Instead I get an impression of elaborate stage lights fastened to a ceiling. They are not switched on. Instead, the same lunar light swirls around me and disappears leaking out from my gut.

A bit further forward, I find I am hanging with both hands onto an airplane ladder, outside, attached to the fuselage. As the plane passes over a landscape, I release my grip on the ladder but don't fall, *held up* by my severed writing-drawing hand.

Seen from the air, visible below, is the freeway…streaming vehicles. The landscape is a light tan color with a lot of planting beside the road. In some places scrolls of sod are stacked, awaiting clarification, to be unfurled later. The further we voyage beyond city limits, the coarser the planting gets…Fronds of giant ferns appear, and big spider plants…When I gaze horizontally across the sky, I am able to observe the zeppelin's duralumin gondola, about the size of a school bus, voyaging

into hinterlands over map green terrain ...

Erewhon

I have entered a square brown building, a house of death and dissection…There could be an air of formaldehyde but there isn't. I am standing on a black dissecting table at the point of being disgusted with the prospect of going over some issues with which I am already familiar when I realize there are others in the room. As I step down from the table, I behold an attractive, almost plump woman dressed to resemble a child. She needs to make a drawing but wants conviction.

However, she shows me preliminaries. The people unresolved but the landscape one I like: a partially logged mountainside.

I tell her I like her picture but she says, "Oh, yeah. *Sounds* right," indicating the picture. She's not quite plump in a way that is attractive though I am not yet drawn to her want of conviction.

Excellent trees for a log house are bulldozed aside to get at what's marketable. I am not consulted. Planted around the burns and heavy slash, fresh green pine seedlings are marketable full grown in thirty years. Only managed 300 seedlings today. The women plant more. No matter how I want to characterize it, at day's end, with boots off, I own aching feet. Age thirty-four. Powerless tree planter.

Back in a city supposedly familiar to me everything looks changed. The room is sunny and bright. The simian at the point where I usually begin to worry because he is perhaps criminal, but this time, for some reason, I don't. A smooth stillness, not amiable, blank, and in another part of the room, a woman in sunlight…I gaze out the window at a river. I no longer believe it is the city I know because there are canal boats and bronze temple bells rotating on the water…Banquet in a hall. She is present though it hardly looks like her: now she is the suntanned model, slender, dressed in red, smiling.

What is fashionable and empty tells me nothing …

I am about to leave the city. The apartment where I have been is blackened and unfamiliar. The stairs are changed too, are still wood but end in a half spiral of planks at the bottom. My room is upstairs and I have come down to an apartment on the ground floor to speak to the man who lives here. He is exactly my age but has no physical characteristics. I have known him all the time I have been living in the city though he is not identifiable with any actual person. I tell him when I leave I will put the key to my room in his mailbox so he can pass it on to the landlord. I notice the key is the key to the mailbox here.

Outside, under an arch, there is a door, and standing just inside it, cut by shadow, two. First I address a banker's son who accuses *me* of giving in too easily without detailing what he means.

Outside…I put my right foot up on a soccer bench to tie my cordovan. Banker's son goes on about being in the movies. As I tie my shoe I question him asking whether he was trained before the passage, a priori, or on the job…He seems to anticipate a conventional negative reaction on my part, jealousy is it?…or anger, but when I wait to see if either is what I actually feel, it isn't.

Fronting the Outback

Next episode occurs within a racially mixed group, near an airport, in an urban area. One of them looks to be a business woman in her forties or fifties, stout, wearing a no-nonsense suit…She tells me that she is the state or city gov't in Illinois. For all I know she may be the governor. Which recalls TM7 and Obey's weedy backyard with its overturned, rusted shopping cart. I remember we stood regarding it out her back door when she remarked, "Doesn't it look like Illinois?"

Again I know she is making a request of me. I must think she still wants something of me. This time I am unclear about the exact nature of her request--to do with 8 1/2 x 11 sheets and the state of city gov't--except this time connects the dots to Disillusioned Journalist and whatever it was a group of prostitutes he was required to interview revealed re gov't rigging. I remember how he went on scribbling vast ntbks 4 himself as a means of displacing local newsprint.

I'm thinking all of this must be an allusion to that ex gov, neither a woman nor black, who I read recently had been indited for graft. Who, before he left office, released a number of inmates from death row after DNA testing revealed they could not possibly have committed the murders which cost them decades.

My bus isn't city but intercity. Line and logo quite strange, not Greyhound…Wide aisles resemble a jumbo jet, crowded; elbows to the left and right. I'm crammed with the seat in front reclined against my knees.

I lean forward to reach over the seat in front to clasp the shoulder of the bus driver who is "of course black." I shake his shoulder, saying, "Wait just one moment…Mr. Bus Driver, stop this bus."

The bus in question is Nivon City and I'm clear about where it stops, on 10th near the top of the hill, near Varsity Cinemateque. (Everybody knows Varsity Cinemateque.) Mercifully, the bus is headed out of the area. I remember a bowling alley, gas station, intersection, cross street before the bus stop with its too familiar bench. Right at the top of the hill was a place where you could sit looking out across the bay at heat-shimmering freighters double parked below …

The bus halts at precisely this spot. I inform the driver, because of the woman's clarified request, he ought to stop and wait until I have my shoes back on because I am just barefoot and there is no such thing as form. People to the left and right are dis-

mwe

gruntled; they want to get moving, turn the page, get on home, get on with their lives, not wait up for somebody like me about to tie on his track record.

With middle-aged, new or newly-excavated assertiveness, I inform them, "Hold your horses. I am tying my shoes and won't expect to hurry." I see shoes to the left of me, beneath the seat in front. I must reach down for them.

My attitude is…take my time. After all, the business woman never was CP's daughter. For that, I owe it to myself whenever her request = a contraction.

To the Cleaners

Whereas, the next building resembles KZZ, community-operated FM station in Nivon City. I have this association with the station: I could be its listener, as well as an unpaid volunteer. I enter one of the rooms inside the station which is bare except for a table. On the table I find a large manila envelope. Inside it are pink slips from a dry cleaning establishment; each slip lists the charge for an article being cleaned. There is an aura of money anxiety. Nobody tells me anything, but it occurs to me the station must be in the middle of a fund raiser. I wonder what exactly could be ongoing. Are people connected with the station getting their garments cleansed gratis? What deal? I proceed from table to counter. A man who still works for the station stands behind it. He is already engaged, talking to a preceding customer, as it were. I have to wait to ask him about dry cleaning slips. As I wait I notice a little box of "memory reels," some type of electronic file 4all those connected with KZZ; it may additionally contain duplicate programs. When I start to check through the file, the man behind the counter somewhat abruptly finishes his exchange with the one who usually precedes me. I ask him about the dry cleaning slips, but the one behind the counter seems suddenly struck dumb, not reticent: unable to speak. He is present, but something--my question, or the one who precedes me--has rendered him mute. I remember now that there used to be a dry cleaning establishment back of where he stands. I remember clothes on wire hangers in plastic bags, also the odor of benzene as you climbed the stairs. Didn't the radio station share the building with a dry cleaners? Or was it visa versa? I remember round windows of big green, tumble-wash dry cleaning machines and a wall behind them painted drab, institutional green.

I ask if the people at the station are getting some break on their cleaning bills. He is unable to respond to my inquiry. He has been rendered speechless by what we are not given to know, or don't care to know. He may or he may not know anything about dry cleaning. In either case, unlike the vociferous gov't, he just can't say.

Waxing reflective, I begin to mull over the history of the phrase "to the cleaners." Meaning that somebody is bested, or you are 1up, or even better.

I first associate the phrase with Mr. C on 8-Ball Island, since it always seemed to be a favorite of his. I remember the day when I departed from 8-Ball, running into Mr. C with his wife, recently returned from Virginia, who appeared to be trying to demonstrate a point of preceding me onto the ferry, although I only happened to be at the gov't dock a minute ahead of him. He neatly elbowed past me carrying several articles of clothing on hangers inside transparent cleaner bags. I greeted him en passant, but he didn't like speaking too much to me. Which may have had something to do with his son who, Soda Lake informed me, died horribly a few years earlier in a work accident. This was after Lad & Dad spent most of the night drinking and shout-arguing about their farm. Next day, working hung over, after being rousted out a few hours early by his drunken father banging a mop handle from below on the floor of his bedroom, the son swung down from his backhoe seat descending into the ditch before him to examine a half-excavated boulder. The ground was soft from night rain; the backhoe slid, tumbling after him, severing his neck, killing him instantly.

While on 8-Ball I tried to get Mr. C to teach me things it would have been helpful to know. Like how to operate a chain saw. He would not. I remember a moment outdoors; we were discussing some farm matter as I loaded alder rounds he had cut into the truck. In the course of our discussion, he faked a gesture. Very stagily and without really smiling, he pretended that his right hand was trembling. At the time I found the gesture puzzling. Later, in Nivon City, I encountered its twin in a foreign language film at Varsity Cinematheque. Everybody knows Varsity Cinematheque. I don't recall the title or plot of the film, but the tale involved an East European farmer whose right hand shook. As I left the theater, I happened to remember a recent discussion Mr. C had had with his wife in my presence. They had just returned to 8-Ball after a mainland visit with their daughter, a journalism major at university. I specifically remember them discussing that particular foreign language series. So, Mr. C had apparently appropriated his trembling hand gesture from a current foreign film.

A few months after this cinematic revelation, I experienced something similar in a $2.00, second run, rundown theater downtown. The theater was frequented mostly by old age pensioners like the ones whose dust-streaked windows I had just finished cleaning with bucket and sponge.

I entered in the middle of the feature which, I gathered, concerned a romantic young couple touring rural Spain in their tiny caravan. Their relationship, though intense, is tenuous. At the end of the journey, after a period of soul searching, they decide to liquidate the caravan and go their separate ways. Nothing remarkable until the heroine's departure speech, which ends with the clinker, "I think we've had the best of it." Internally, a gong sounded. I went to the lobby for a coffee. As I sat drinking it, I thumbed through the first indelible year in Nivon City, to the 2nd place I rented from a Mrs. CG, whose romance had ejected early. After downsizing, knowing full well he lacked anything to write home about, her husband had returned across the pond to the isle of their birth. She found herself parked on this side with a mortgage and 1 infant son to raise.

At the time I thumbed back to, Nadia Concepción and I were still seeing each other regularly and sessionally. Even during that transitional period, I didn't imagine her visits would threaten or upset any apple carts. Mrs.

CG had assured me when I forked over the first month's rent that it would be no problem if Nadia were occasionally to spend the night. I was paid up always and am not naturally loud, but one evening after another day labor stint, I was fumbling with the key at my cellar door when she called down to me from the tiny porch outside her kitchen. I stepped back to look up. Mrs. CG leaned upon the balustrade to deliver a mysterious and seemingly practiced speech. Her black hair, usually up, was deplaited; she wore a quilted robe of oriental design. As she launched into what sounded like a well-honed routine, I was able to decifer only that she had reversed her judgement on girl friends overnight and that I was meant to depart. What registered as peculiar, after the initial shock, was that she seemed to be addressing somebody "over there." She didn't look at me but at a distant corner of her backyard, at eggshells piled on top of the compost heap. I knew she drank a little; beer bottles rattled occasionally outside her door, but she didn't seem to have been drinking. I heard her painfully pronouncing antique phrases such as "out-of-the-way affair." Her notice seemed scripted and mysteriously adjacent to my present circumstance. It ended with a recontextualized clinker: "I think we've had the best of it."

A few years later, in the lobby of the run-down, 2nd run downtown, I pondered how many times she would have had to sit through that particular B film to get the heroine's lines by heart.

Contract

Old garments, stripped to rags, quite a few of them, are strewn in two ploughed fields, in furrows, with a spine corridor, or aisle, down the middle …

I am *nothing but*…an old homeless vagrant wearing thick padded clothes. Beside the parked electrocycle, I sleep in a covered doorway on 4th. In the morning I wake lost in padded clothes,

preparing to return to the house on 3rd.

Hitchhiking, I stop near the big field to the right of the road where a New Age film, "No Obligatory Sequence," is being reshot. During a break I manage to engage the ingenue taking part in the film. We wander up a hill to a spot just below some trees. My hand is upon her when technicians from Production call her back into it.

Now it seems the tour group is not a film unit, but an agricultural commune, out in the same ragged fields. A man in a checkered shirt speaks to the group seated on folding chairs. To the right of folding chairs…is one of the commune's vegetable gardens between a rail fence and a shed. The vegetables include a large cauliflower which is quite fragrant…It's odor pervades the assembly. Someone hands around pictures of a shack where their leader lived amid pine barrens. A rough shack though clearer inside than you might expect.

With arms out-stretched, I fly weight-edly down from a mountain. I can see a narrow highway a-stream with cars, passing below…Then I have touched down… Another short hop and I am preparing to

cross a border…Now there is a woman with me who is invisible…As we enter a small maze to-gether, I experience a sense of antique Romance I assumed had been destroyed by experience.

Following the maze we are right at a border where we discover quite a heap of rags. Over yonder is a border guard who may give us trouble. I pick up a sample of shredded rags and whisper to Invisible that she should do the same. If we evaluate, or appear to be evaluating these rags, the border guard won't bother us.

Meantime back at Rice Jungle, the room

claimed by my brother and his wife has become a gym inside. On the floor nothing but padded gym mats, clean, gray-white, though torn. Again there is an aura of clean rags.

I climb down to sit cross-legged on a mat before I stand with a window on my left, leaning on Interior Commitment's dresser of light-colored wood. There is a bag of dark green homegrown on the dresser. After rolling one, I remember rolling a number before that I ate since I had no matches.

I look outside, remembering Mrs. C's yard level with the rented basement…Just behind my left shoulder is another window with a dark-haired woman inside who is watching me. The leaded glass in the door to the side porch forms a diamond net or grid. On the narrow strip of grass just beyond shrubs that surround the Hermes Crescent porch, I confront a lurking_____? Creature? From the Black Lagoon? Push it away.

The chair back in the rented room is exerpted

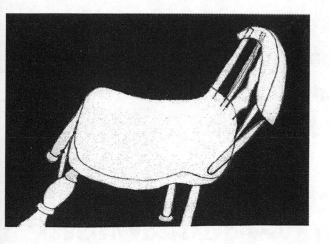

from my drawing of it, separated from the body of the chair. I grasp the segment firmly in both hands in case I need to give somebody a shove.

I look away for an instant. When I look back, the girl from a summer birthday party has disappeared. Occupying her space is

a composite beast. That friend of Interior Commitment, who went south for work in a boatyard after failing in the Capitol- -due to "faulty place-of-birth"--has combined with a reptile- headed turtle/snake, which is the mosaic I reassembled on the 8 1/2 x 11 wall of my 8 1/2 x 11 room from 8 1/2 x 11 sheets …

Behind the creature, the lattice skirtiing

the family's summer cottage, up on posts, unlatches into an area where old lumber is stored, where I excavate torn bits of a scary monster comic, the one I shredded when eight years old.

I don't recall the plot exactly but remember the scary part had to do with a veiled old lady in black who died in her wheelchair. Her relatives went on pretending she was alive for some reason to do with a plot mechanism that was intended to supply forward momentum in lieu of development. Strangers couldn't say she wasn't alive because of the veil and because each relative did their level best to speak for their deceased ancestor. (Many relatives = a number of gospels, so a lot of people got work.) The cell of the black-veiled old woman, pushed forward in her creaking wicker wheelchair by a dependant relative, scared me so badly I refused to reread the comic despite Unhelpful's dare, choosing instead to dismember the issue, shredding it to confetti behind the summer lattice, under her porch.

Returned to that spot, my vehicle has vanished. Again I peer out beneath porch stairs into bright sunlight…Now grainy walls of the tiny rented room seem to swirl around me like a cape, leaving barely room to turn …

A white explosion. Movement away from it; crossing the B Street Bridge, I look left toward a village in the country near Rice Jungle where I have returned with a Negro boy on my left. In the village a clothing store has been damaged by fire. No one is around when we go inside where the clothes are rummaged through and look rumpled. A fire sale is indicated even though the clothes are undamaged and there is no smoke smell. I pick up a chambray shirt with a funny pointed collar. I find a turtleneck for myself and …

2 brunettes. One just slightly older has shoulders round *like* the young one, which is quite becoming.

So to the tune of a rag being torn, a field is parted evenly by a road through the middle, leading up to an ancient memory locus. Now the surrounding fields turn to dust…I wander naked in two fields bathed in reddish dust…A sister approaches across the fields in a flesh-colored body stocking, age around twenty. She comes toward me, warning of the approach of 2 enormous, eyeless kangaroos. I may have to box or spear them. But they have departed. Are we standing near a fence?…Anyway, we proceed toward the house and climb a ladder onto the roof before entering it through a dormer window. I tell her I think it would be a good idea to build wooden steps into the roof. She agrees. It's a metal roof, reddish maroon color…Inside we proceed toward the metal typing table.

Looking up from a page as if for approval, Nadia Concepción crys despairingly she might just as well spend every cent on clothes.

A beautiful woman peels off her clothes, beginning at the waist. She knocks on the door of the house before spraying black from her waist at one who opens the door …

Earlier, traveling on a bus with musicians, I had not forgotten I was hungover; woke, felt around for the duocello; saw it; saw Culture-by-Committee. I had to separate her out from the group. Only her. Then outside, I walked with her and her friend (her body). She had been persuaded to wear a trace of lipstick since her waist remained pure. I carried her up a dark staircase toward a room. She was easy to carry. In the corridor doctors mill around like a hospital. I carry her to the room.

Now I see that a woman on stage is garbed in white. Though her clothes keep changing, becoming longer, shorter, squarer…the cloth from which they are cut remains the same.

Getting off a boat, ferry, or an airplane I proceed over a bridge with the woman I love but have never met on my left. Her face turns so I see just the profile. I have a white, telescoping cane which I crumple and drop over the railing. It lands at the top of a pier down near a sprig of weeds. When I brush against her, in particular, I wake very happy.

Then Uses Milk, again, though not her. I touch pale breath. Her moon deflates suddenly, wooshing around and around like a toy, before it drops in a corner.

Over such familiar ground, covered with familiar snow, I pursue the girl with the sled. I myself have a kayak I am using in place of a sled. Right where the snow bank edges the School for 1 drive, she takes off down hill...I start to follow with the kayak before telling her, "No, I don't go that way." I turn and start back up hill. She turns, abandoning her sled, and starts to follow me back up...Up top she takes my arm and we walk together across the athletic field into a courtyard. She is English now; smiles with big horse teeth, though her ankles curve forward like M's.

I have to ask if it's preset that a homebuilt cigarbox blues zither only play blues?

No.

When a sheet of writing has been slid beneath the strings, a folk singer dressed in white or, alternatively, in white; sings and strums, strums and sings from the JV stage of JV gym. People in the audience are supposed to be talking about her paramount style. Is it jazz? She is singing not words. Her singing turns into laughter. She = singing laughter. Again I am awakened by my own laughter.

Looking into the next room, I witness a man. Trying to sound at once tough and smart, I tell him, "That's the way it is, baby." Then I notice--while I am being flippant--two others have made off with my shoes. So, I'm supposed to sort through a bunch of theirs, looking for my own, which of course I fail to find. So, I am barefoot, like atypical debooted POW, Xpendably directed behind enemy lines.

Abruptly returned to Construe, I drive my vehicle along S. Ave. toward W. St. At the top of the hill I open the car door and start to get out. I am still barefoot, though behind my seat, or just under it, I discover a pair of steel-toed shit-kickers I could have used in Nivon City. Impulsively, about to go the extra mile, I start across the street. With a will of its own, the vehicle surges forward, door still open. Somehow my spine snaps me back into the driver's seat; and as the car jerks forward, slamming the door, we rapidly turn a corner.

I have motored back to this remote memory locus. Outside, on a rounded elevation, my brother moves amid a group of daughter-like girls in school uniforms with pleated skirts attempting to address them. There is another girl, not in uniform--in clinging white, with white-blond hair. She dances toward me near Bungalow Mansion doing rapid pirouettes. As I approach her, I try to coax her into the mansion. She hesitates. She doesn't want to enter the mansion just yet, if ever. I wait impatiently, not trying to force her.

To kill time and stay awake, Mother and I

perambulate out of doors. Two expensive military jets pass overhead. On the left almost camouflaged by trees are several open railroad cars, like coal cars. One of the military planes is supposed to have plopped an ICBM into a railroad car for storage but when I pull myself up to stare down inside, it's empty.

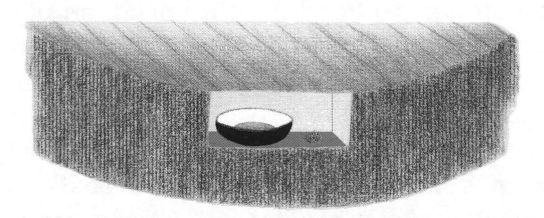

In the mansion I take a stand at the sink in a renewed effort to purify her dishes…A performance is ongoing as I stand down below the stage in the front row "prompter" area where a dish washing niche is cut out of the stage edge and a bowl inset in it. I stay myself by *not* empathizing with Unhelpful as I scoop bits of scouring pad and potato fragments out of the bowl to fling to the right where two curtains part, revealing a young, black woman, apparently a maid, who stands disrobed. She begins speaking foreign languages. Greek, or to do with Greek. (Antisthenes.) I turn immediately to Mother and say, "Just look at our maid. She's taken off all her clothes." Another maid, an older white woman, standing near outside the curtains, says, "Oh, no, you shouldn't have told her."

Ideas-per-Second "improves" mysteriously. I am seated beside her. Her breasts are revealed. As her older self strolls around behind my shoulder blade, a shred of paper is exchanged between the two before Ideas covers hers, only to reveal them again once the older woman has departed. I express some feelings and see Ideas-per-Second's hair change to blond, then back to black. "No. No," she says, ejecting me.

Into a square pool, like a Eureka tub. I have

a small piece of board I take with me into the vertical pool. A moment later when I get out to change my clothes, there is a line dividing my body evenly in two. So, the eyes of the little girl of about four or five are chalk. She has grown weary of scrutiny, and unless I can get her to empathize with greater clarity, it seems they will continually attempt to off her…For encouragement, I rub her lower back.

In the 1930s jazz club, I wear black evening clothes and am my father. A black cornettist is about to perform in front of the orchestra. The other, who remains within, points out that the trumpet player's clothes are ragged and inferior and, in many respects, deficient. He suggests we each strip off some cloth to improve the musician's outfit before he goes on stage. The other removes his jacket. I maintain a fig leaf while unraveling my tie.

Now I can see myself in a mirror, from the side, and think for a minute, there is no arm attached to my right shoulder, but when I look again, there is, and the moment I see my arm, I am born upward beyond the mirror …

Late, I marry a lean brunette in her mid-forties who enters our bedroom wearing a diamond choker and sleeveless black dress. After a tough day I return from the office tired. She asks if we are still going to the party. I see she thinks we ought to go so I say all right, although I am tired. She comes on to me, but it's possible she is faking. We lie naked on the bed, talking, before changing our clothes. She rolls weightedly off and falls with a thud between 2 beds.

Off a narrower room with a lot of windows and sunny weather outside, there is an even smaller room where Ideas-per-Second is sitting with others. Her anger has something to do with my neice. At this juncture I discover a small optic device. An eyepiece with a larger and a smaller lens. When I peer through it, nothing is magnified or brought any closer, but the light seems better organized; i.e., polarized.

This is most likely because each morning I dress for work. My problem is my clothes are deficient. For a shirt I can muster only a nylon rain jacket with a collar like a shirt. I imagine I could wear my sweater over it with the collar out. For shoes I have only slippers. As I start to flip flop down stairs I am worried my clothes won't be right on the job. I meet Leg-Up, Jr., returning. He is presently sampling another plum to see if it is precisely to his taste. On the way up, he waxes more boisterous than Foreign Language Student, seeming to believe he has aced the big one, the big test. Descending, I peer out a window, noting the JV school bus which is here to pick me up for temp work.

For a pass time, a grave or pit is dug in earth. The woman's corpse is wrapped in gauze. Her head newly separate from her body. I crouch beside her and a book buried with her. In the two-sided room with others, an Egyptian mummy stays wrapped and prone on its stone slab as we proceed to the second half where a flickering projector projects "Isolated Islet Adventure."

I wander amid trees.

I see another in white with a white cloth around her head who is American and familiar though I can't remember how it was I met her

before language. There is a red ink smudge on her forehead and sweatband. Something about the way she notices permits recall of damp jeans I handed her freshly laundered. Because I have been "helpful" again, I am angry with myself. She appears concerned about whether or not she should wear her jeans slightly damp and let them dry adhered for the best possible fit.

On my behalf I proceed to an address in the West End to see about construction similar to G-Isle townsite. Usually others are scheduled ahead of me. Folded neatly over one arm I carry a pair of khakis I have not put on though I am by no means naked. In my other hand I have the red lobster from Isolate Island, cooked, but still wriggling. While we await the hiring boss, I toss the creature into a black rubber bucket to watch it scurry around and around. When the straw boss arrives we find out the work is part-time. I would still earn too much to remain solvent, so I remove the lobster from the bucket and drop it into deep, cold water.

The religious kult involves Xpendables; i.e., human sacrifice. Victims willing to offer themselves for a million dollars are slain in front of worshippers. Afterward their bodies, wrapped in mummy rags, are deposited in "aluminium tubes."

I try out the schizophrenic district to see about cutting the grass. I apply myself inside a long building consisting of many rooms. There is something sleazy about the man who takes my application. He will cut part of the lawn around a church across the street and leave the mower running for me to finish the job…A volunteer leads me through several rooms and seems interested in me though, as before, she may be feigning. We cross over to the church passing, as we climb some steps, a statue of a woman made of logs beside a statue of a woman made of shit.

Held on with only a few leather carpet tacks,

the clothes trunk lid opens a couple of inches like the kitchen window. Can't see much in there except grayness. It must be father's old trunk from the musty room off the B Blvd garage. I remember it contained his moth-eaten, olive drab uniform, the one I thought I would wear but was told, "No, it's moldy," so the trunk remained shut.

When I remember power I associated with his clothes, a heavy, large, blond woman is slain. Her corpse has already begun to disintegrate. The face is fuzzy. She lies in cool dirt beneath the summer cottage. Who is she? I've never seen her before. I find her exactly where I shredded the scary monster comic. A pile of lumber is stacked nearby to keep it dry. I wake terrified. Am I the murderer? I feel light but weighted.

A worm = the person who has been killed. An earthworm I once threw off a rainy sidewalk into grass. There is a Biblical quotation as I slice the worm into tiny pieces I try at first to bury in snow but can't because the snow has frozen hard. I remember that cruel kid who tore a worm apart as the rest of us watched. Somebody said each twisting piece would sprout into a new worm.

I go to the back of the house with the worm pieces carefully cupped in my hands. Voice-over explains ceremoniously about the pieces I throw into the yard. I still feel guilty about the imaginary murder. Voice-over cites a Biblical passage: you don't know when your hour is come, any moment could be your last, so take no thought about what you will eat, drink, or wear. (Don't worry about a month's rent.) Don't concern yourself. You shouldn't dwell on anything in this life.

I bury worm pieces in the dirt.

Later, in a large, plush hotel, some folks I'm with abandon me; descend in the elevator to the street where I may meet up with them *after* I find my cloth, which I left somewhere in the hotel. I walk through elegant dining rooms and chandelier'd ballrooms but can't find any clothes. I'm naked from the waist. The rich guests don't notice; too busy turning, posturing, pushing in chairs under elegant women who smile cooly. The girl who works inside says she'll show me where my garments are. I follow her into the Hearst cinema which is part of the hotel. She doesn't show me a thing but sits with her boyfriend necking in the back row. I sit to watch disposable films.

One so dumb I hesitate to mention; "World's Narrowest Store," in Nivon City, which I remember was always changing hands. In this instance it's become a fur store specializing in men's furs. The owner's slinky wife appears in billboard advertisements, being handled by a well-known celebrity seated in a corner of the store…What am I doing here? I did not order a fur coat, could not afford one even if I had. I am wearing my war resister's field jacket recently back from the cleaners. I ask the sales girl if I can try on a coat. I do not want a fur coat but it is as if this procedure were an item to be crossed off a list. Mercifully, the sales girl does not trust me. She thinks I may be a thief and says I may look at coats, but not try one on. (A sigh of peace.)

At times many might suspect that there are but two rooms, a rich room--which is more or less of a hall--and a poor room with cardboard walls. In the poor room, a party of grotesques, mostly older folks, stands around drinking. I am seated on the bed examining a "new" white shirt of imitation silk, shopworn, dusty, still in its wrapper, purchased decades ago... Out in the hallway rich guests are putting on and taking off coats.

Far away I hear the sound of a party which my mother is attending. I instruct two small Negro boys to gut the room. They strip cardboard off the walls...Then mother appears to gather up scraps of cloth and lace, which she salvages, before returning to the party.

Drunk myself, I appear in a lecture hall, staring up at the space where the lecturer's podium should be. In place of the lectern there is a child's play house with cloth and sewing materials inside. Next I see a woman in a bright calico dress. Her face so bright my own head is turned to one side. When she notices I'm drunk, she starts to gather her sewing materials rapidly and maybe fearfully. I blurt out she has nothing to fear.

Again, I'm in the backseat, but somehow I've been driving. Or is that just my "ego projection"? I get out at a stop, open the back door and reach inside to sort through clothes and rags strewn across the floor and back seat…I pick out a pair of sweat-sticky socks, the kind I was required to peel from the feet of alcoholics when I worked at a skid row health clinic …

Prior to her latest…bon voyage, Mother and

I enter a European ship cabin. After a few glasses of champagne, she is in the mood to scamper back into her glad rags and unbuckled red galoshes. The floor is scattered with papers, and there are drawers flung open. Today, experiencing multiplicity, she is nervous and unsteady...and I...steady her.

At last I am recalled by two antique childhood dreams...In the first, red brocade dragons pulse and swim in spirals: *Chinese* before I knew the word Chinese. In the second, I crawl through brush tunnels bordering the field of rags until I am able to stand inside a brush cave which dissolves into clear azure at the moment that chanting begins ...

Islet in a Blizzard

So I've passed through the arch--lined with shelves of well-thumbed dream journals--into the Hermes Crescent living room in Construe.

Although the living room I remember was good-sized, there is a sense that it is now confined. Something has shrunk the room as if furniture or other items in storage, which remain invisible, were piled up very close to me. There is one in the way I can see, a cloth-covered stool which I remember formed the pedestal beneath our portable b&w TV. There is also a boxer in the room, a miniaturized Cassius Clay. He is about my height, age 7 or 8. I have hired him to give me boxing lessons. I've already paid but seem to have forgotten that I hired him. He shows up and puts up his dukes so I put up mine. I figure since I've already paid I may as well have the lesson. We each lace up a single boxing glove of a pair like that time boxing with Uses Milk's kid when he was about to divorce her before he returned to der vaterland.

Earlier I had knelt on the floor to dub a music tape, which shrunk me to the height of miniaturized Cassius. We were about to commence with the lesson when I bumped into the cloth-covered TV stool behind me. I was trying to move the stool out of the way to make room for the lesson when something changed…The boxer disappeared, stool disappeared, and I was left with a slip of paper in my hand, folded into tiny pieces. Perhaps it was that contractual shred exchanged, behind my shoulder blade, between Ideas-per-Second and her older self. I unfolded the letter (actually only a note) which read:

> "In the year 187? in_____, Alaska, a blizzard went on for hours, more than a day, both day and night, and for x hours falling snow made it impossible to separate day from night."

While kneeling on the floor dubbing music, I was leafing, at intervals, through a book of Chinese drawings and calligraphy. One of a series of "album leaves" from the 18th century by an artist whose name I don't recall. Each of the paintings I found accompanied by a fragment of calligraphy. Of the few translated fragments one paired the artist's poem with a somewhat standard rendition of a branch of plum blossoms...The poem for the drawing

described a tiny Chinese island newly effaced by remote blizzard.

Want of Conviction

. .the worst / Are full of passionate intensity."

--W.B. Yeats

I walk barefoot toward our house. If it were a drawing it would fill the width of the page to the margin. At first I seem to be approaching the

back courtyard of the house in Construe, except that the courtyard is bordered now on both sides by walkways of cast concrete blocks 4-5 ft above the courtyard. As I walk toward the house there is a door above me at the level of my head. I walk barefoot toward it. Again my awareness is focused on my feet. I see that they are enlarged and somewhat flatter than usual. They resemble Sherpa's feet but are still my feet. They are also "the teacher's feet." I see that these feet are dirty and over gritty. There are a few pools of water I step into to wash off the grit. The ground is composed of cinders like cinders for a cinder track with small clear puddles in the cindery ground. I try to wash off the grit before stepping up onto the walkway to enter the house. On the walkway I observe that the house seems to have a glass door slid back and that there are sliding screens like the pool house in K …

The episode continues at the top of a high, truncated, Mexican-type pyramid. There is a platform at the top of the pyramid 20-30 ft square where I encounter the man I think I should help, who typically precedes me. Emaciated, he is about my height. Though I can't see his face, I think he is E. Indian, hair and skin dark. The main thing about him is unsteadiness, like me madre toward the end of our contract. Multiplicity is taxing his balancing ability and he needs me to steady him. He is no longer drunk but may be ill. He wears pointy shoes and seems to be swiveling on his feet, left and right from the ankles in a kind of jittery dance step that Obeys-her-Friends would have approved at one point. As if he were to say, "Please help! I'm near collapse. I'm dizzy and may be ill."

He falls and I grab him under the armpits to drag him in through the door at the top of the pyramid. Inside there is a hospital, very narrow. I support him, helping him to a couch which is like a couch in the common, TV-viewing area of a 1950s women's dormitory. Without the TV, however...Couch is dilapidated and indented as if someone had recently flopped there. A few clean clothes, a jacket, and socks have been left behind. It's like I were back at the skid row health clinic and he were my neediest patient. I help him to lie down on the couch and lift his feet up with his head resting on a folded pillow. I hurry off to find the doc because he seems quite ill. If he is a teacher, it is strictly in the academic sense; yes, it seems now that he has morphed into an E. Indian academic.

Near Miss (Very Becoming)

Meantime, goingback4 Nivon City in my car… makes it difficult to say much re indirection… If I had been a bit more aggressive, or slightly less so. If I had omitted a word, or expanded the context even slightly, I *can* help thinking she might of reacted differently…After all, except for one afternoon, she never actually liked me. For, I still think in images, and am not that tall. Despite character flaws, at that time

I lacked gainful employment. Also, she had been lead to believe that the onus for antiwar research lay mostly on those of my ilk, whose fathers remain throughout their lives without any taint of redundancy.

With me, inside the vehicle nobody commands, on my left, is Inferior Commitment in the guise of an indiscriminant pop consumer, who remains nonetheless one of her staunchest allies.

Our vehicle is double-parked on a side street separating the Big Scoop ice cream parlor (journalism student's hangout) from Varsity Cinemateque…Now I remember that that particular street ran across 10th to a little park with a lookout over Freighter Bay.

At night, inside the vehicle, waiting for the ticket window to reopen, we used to analyze and reanalyze Compulsion's Plum. Inferior tries to misdirect me about her only child he says was named Elizabeth, the name of our cook in Construe. Memory serves, however. I know for a fact CP had a single child, a son who liked drawings I found washed up on Brickbat Beach, along the shore.

I remember one evening, as I exited from the Cinemateque, running into her in the queue, electrified, lined up for the second showing of a foreign language series. She was with a man a few decades older, emphasized by the white frock she wore; maybe a little girlish, for her, though becoming. I think she would have been around thirty at the time.

In the lineup she greeted me matter-of-factly, requesting my reaction to the avant-garde film, which I can't now recall, much less what I might have mumbled in reply. What's perfectly clear is the sentence I should have whispered, in passing, in her left ear …

East of the theater, I reencounter the man behind the desk as I am about to buy a 2nd ticket, and reenter. I experience a lack of focus trying to relocate the address. I have a notion the theater must have moved 6-8 blocks east, around the corner on 10th.

I talk to the man behind the desk who has apparently studied the problem. He tries to tell me that there are 2 theaters and wants me to believe he has schedules for both. He lays the schedules on the desk in front of him, turned around for me to read. I am as positive that there is only 1 theater as I am that CP had a single child, a son who liked drawing, not a girl named Elizabeth. I haven't time for 2 schedules, wandering now inside a strangely familiar building with the information desk at the top or bottom of escalator stairs. There are people walking around contained by their work in this large building consisting of plate glass offices and stores…It's toward the end of the day when nearly everyone is headed for homework.

I approach a steel table with a stack of paper plates on it like the cafeteria table in the hospital before my mother's death. I don't buy anything. I rest my chin on the stack of paper plates. Folks who smilingly claim they don't know nothing dash around busily. One man is singing and--if

I can read his thoughts--concocting lyrics for a fellow office worker, a woman he loves. It's all pretty vague and familiar; which indicates I ought to refuse to try or not try.

The episode deadends as I emerge from the brush tunnel of my drawing--the one bordering the field at the bottom of Hermes Crescent in Construe--though in this episode it has moved near Varsity Cinemateque in Nivon City.

I'm on a unicycle, one-wheeled vehicle which, in this case, has no seat; but is made

to resemble a pogo stick. You stand on pedals attached directly to the wheel. Pole is sheered off near the top sharply like …

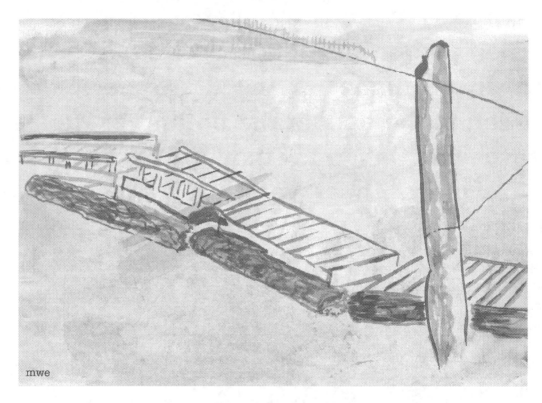

mwe

"You look about fifteen," I would have said.

Encased in Earwax

Mistaken-for-Plainclothes was the friend who deserted from the army about the time that I launched my career as a draft dodger. From bits and pieces of my account circulating in *Chaff* ('82) and *iota* ('91), you've undoubtedly pieced it together that we both eroded, fleeing to and then from Test Market 7, during that ancient era. Probably I ought to "reinvent better name" now that Mistaken has morphed into a man of the cloth. I can't help wondering in what way he recovered his garment of eternity. From the last letter I received all I understand is he is a minister these days.

In an historical sense, one should forgive but--once a lesson is learned--never forget... One I can't seem to forget is C.E., a different near miss, who, at a certain point in Test Market 7, was favorably disposed toward each of us, though, in the end, she inclined toward him. What I mean to evoke is not jealousy so much as an encroaching sense of arbitrariness. Evidently, telos may not be absent just because I don't know how to look for it. Maybe telos is looking for me.

As though there could be an ilk, what happened exactly?

After living as a subterranean army deserter for too long, after coast-to-coast tripping on fake credit cards, Mistaken wound up back in Metropolis, where he made a decision to turn himself in under the amnesty work program. For deserting the shared fictions of Quag I, society should have hung a medal on him. But as he wrote me--back when anything might've been gained through an exchange of letters--he had become convicted of his need for a leg up.

The war instigators formed the guilty party, but it was Mistaken who signed their confession. Faux guilt empowered double whammy to live and propagandize another day. $$ had him expiating their sin, stepping it out as a school inspector in a black ghetto where he was mistakenly viewed as "Mistaken-for-Plainclothes," a covert narc.

Signing their confession got him off Isolated Island all right, but he found that he still had a few problems, that in this so-called war the literal battlefield is just the tip of the iceberg, and that--as they say--life is what you make of it. Every extra cent of a school inspector's paycheck he found himself journaling to the well-recommended Freudian with an old-fashioned leather couch. Together they proceeded through "a rather classical analysis," not so much of our military-industrial quagmire, but of himself. Especially, he wrote me, they had to work through his relationship with his father.

Mistaken's father, who had served for many years as a highly-placed administrator of academe, died during analysis or shortly thereafter, but not before Mistaken was able to avail himself of paternal influence to shoe himself into divinity school…C.E., that near miss, or her afterimage, may be skewing my account somewhat at this point but only insofar as key and shading. The characteristic points remain that Mistaken's father was a highly-placed academic administrator. That his son, an army deserter who had done undergraduate work, without obtaining a degree, gained admission to the graduate program of a prestigious divinity school. Mistaken-for-Plainclothes has gone on to reconstitute himself as a reverend in a New England village.

Near miss appears to remind me that on securing my own undergraduate degree I had an opportunity to attend the same divinity school, which then would have provided a

2-year deferment from the draft. However flatulent it might sound today, my calling at that time inclined toward belated confrontation, rather than divinity school. A career as a draft doger was opening out...In retrospect, on certain days when the endless highway seems merely endless, I must question those youthful enthusiasms...Probably this is no more than nostalgia for a regular pattern of life in accord with an earlier less volatile mode.

In the present episode I have placed Mistaken-for-Plainclothes on a higher level than myself, most likely because of C.E. and because of his career, which even under different circumstances could never have been mine...In the episode in question, he is on a dais a foot above the rest of the room so that I must look up to him, if only slightly. I see, though, that he has become encased in a strange encumbrance, a type of shell made of hard wax--actually more like sealing wax than hardened earwax--which makes him resemble a human chess piece, probably bishop. (With his get up & go he is likely destined for *arch*bishop.) Inside the vertical encasement he may be engaged in an activity occurring outside. There appear to be holes in the encumbrance large enough for him to get his arms and hands through. He has a knife or is it a reamer, of some description, and he is using the instrument to scrape around and around in the holes to enlarge them, ream them out, and eventually, crack the damn thing off him to be rid of the "mundane shell." He appears irascible, or plain angry, as he scrapes.

In future I don't expect I'll hear much from Mistaken though I may hear more about him. From what he last wrote he considers me to be a type of hold out. I am associated in his mind with "the nightmare years" that, in his case, were transcended decades ago. As for the god of this world, AKA father of lies, you maybe know better than I that *his* prime concern remains staying in business.

's Recurrence

Again, I'm back in place of birth, though I sense it's many years prior to my birth. Walking along, the city buildings look old. Some very old, some 3-4 decades ago. Lost, I don't recognize what section of Construe I am in. I have a metal cane which is like a spoon hammered flat for spreading soft margarine in a sandwich shop.

A Negro man walks toward me. I continue to approach him, although from a distance he appears to be a tough guy. I have decided not to be afraid. It developes he isn't all tough but turns into another street...I walk around a thick black tree that has pushed up through the sidewalk, heaving aside concrete …

Now I have entered the narrower street of an impoverished section. There are a few white women outdoors. The architecture of the buildings draws me. I wish I had brought a cardboard returnable so I could make a preliminary snap. Hard to say what interests me about these buildings…Large green tarpaper shingles are plastered kind of loosely over walls and roofs. Though they have not been applied uniformly, the shingles appear not to have been used to cover indifferent joinery or holes in the roof. There is a small church on the street covered with the same green shingles with weedy summer vines growing over it as well. Not grape vines but weed vines with big leaves. Other sunny foliage is shading the church like a Jonah booth and looks as though it ought to be pruned back …

A little further on I look across from a cool night section I have entered to a section where street lights go on…I am walking amid a crowd of people. It seems to be late 1880s judging by the fashions…Another black man, but in a dusty 3-piece suit and bowler hat approaches, asking for money. I give him a special dime, which glows soft white, a contemporary dime stamped with recent date. Time period must be long ago because he appears happy with 10cents. I tell him the dime is special and he should take it to a coin store. He doesn't realize what it's worth, doesn't understand its future. Because of the date, a coin store would certainly consider it an unusual find. He smiles as he walks off examining the coin.

I move toward street lights.

I feel lost, though not depressed. Just as for Mistaken the "nightmare years" have ended, for me, this must not become another "depression era." Though all is strange my aim is to locate the familiar part of town.

Near a lighted street I ask a woman how to get to S. Ave., a nice looking woman in a

1940s dress. Early 1940 *before* the war, not early war years. There is an S-shaped street that snakes back and forth, side to side, uphill from where we stand to another street at a higher level. I ask her if the S-shaped street is B. Boulevard. "No, that's N. Ave." Apparently everybody knows N. Ave. I thank her and tell her I myself know N. Ave; it's the street where my aunt and uncle used to live. At this, she walks away from me, heading for her reliable coupe. She remembers exactly where she parked it and has no difficulty finding it.

I've only started up the S-shaped street toward N. Ave. but at least it's a street I'm familiar with. I'm definitely in Construe's past, as yet it's no particular decade. I try to understand why the past of the man I gave the dime to was much further back than the past of the woman who inadvertently gave me directions.

Flight into Egypt, Or, Sounds in the Ink

"My God, if only something of this could be shared. But would it be then; would it be?"
--Malte Laurids Brigge, (not) Rilke

From my waist up I'm outside, standing in a manhole with the iron lid removed; my lower half is below street level. The  area beneath the street is filled to within 2 or 3 feet of the surface by layers of greasy green bags stuffed with garbage. I stand treadingly on spongy bags of trash which layer out in all directions beneath the street.

It's like summers ago in Test Market 7. The garbage men went on strike during a hot and sticky season. This forced people to take their own sacks to a nearby park where we sandbagged them in orderly pyramids. Within a week fly swarms and a rotting reek had materialized.

Standing in the manhole, on the spongiform layer, I'm conversing with an older woman, like the one in the computer store yesterday. I remember that the sound of her voice seemed to precede anything we spoke about…She moved around behind my shoulder blade. I didn't see her but could hear her talking…What she is saying has to do with not trying to understand in words too soon. The notion of waiting for words to arrive unbidden is a "slowed-down, sentient assembly line to dissect the war economy."

With no transfer or transition I have reboarded the MacD St. bus at the same corner as the manhole, 4th and MacD, where a drugstore was in Nivon City. I find myself seated on the aisle. Facing across it to the other side, I notice a young Chinese girl, very pretty, of the type Leg-Up the Elder once drunkenly admitted he found irresistible. I place the palm of my hand along one side of her face. She mentions an exchange of letters, asking what benefit, if any, I might hope to derive from correspondence. At this time what's given seems more emphatic than what obtained before. I shouldn't try to understand in words right off the bat, but should intuit process and let it unfold at its own rate.

Very next episode interrupts a bustling cafeteria like one in *Milk Bottle H*, yet vaster, more like Blanc Cafeteria in Nivon City. Steam tables where you get trays and food are central; you can completely circumnavigate the steam tables.

A group of starling-sized songbirds, 15-20 of them, have penetrated the room. Peeping and cheeping, they dart around, hop on the floor, take off, fly again. When I examine them I see they are two colors. Black and white. Wings white; breast black; or breast is white and wings black. Some way, alternating, black and white. My reaction is to release them out of doors.

Which corresponds to releasing those birds that used to get trapped inside the rusted, humid, dripping glass pool house in K. In winter they would enter when a gust lifted the ventilator flaps in front of the stilled electric fan, up near the roof. They used to fly around inside bamming into glass walls and would sometimes knock themselves unconscious. Some I manage to catch, as gently as possible, in a bath towel, to release back outside. If the unconscious ones had not self-destructed, a drop of whiskey from an eye dropper might serve to revive them.

The door to the present cafeteria, unlike the old airport cafeteria, is double with a boxlike "mud room" between to keep winter out. I hold open the doors and shoo blackwhite cheepers outside.

Inside, to my left, I look down. The visual element begins to wax indefinite. Nearly Chinese. I notice a charcoal gray area. Something is present I can't quite make out. When I reach toward it with my left hand, I experience first a prickling sensation, bright like thorns, needle-sharp. I pick up whatever it is. Kind of resembles a starfish or sea creature. Like an octopus against aquarium glass when the tentacles pair back rippling. The creature flexes. A ripple spreads from the center all the way around. Blooms rippling from the center. When the creature blossoms outwardly, what follows is difficult to describe. A play of multiples = multiplicity.

I have an inkling of the quality of love my mother gave me, to which is attached the memory of what occurred yesterday as I was having my driver's license photocopied in the rental office. To my right on the other side of the counter, a Southern black woman put away house keys in a sectioned drawer. As I waited for the first one who had taken my license into the back room, the woman sorting keys began talking out loud to herself, going on at length about "Why, Joseph, why?" saying she would be in church tonight (a weekday night). I had to ask myself if I was being conned or was witnessing genuine glossolalia…Her eyes did not roll back in her head; she continued to sort tagged keys; she seemed to be in the throes of a story neither group can tell when both want to allude to it.

The other clerk, also a black woman, returned with my photocopy and began speaking to a man on my left, on my side of the counter, something about the local pentecostal.

Sensation to the present episode is non-verbal. Sense of 3-4-5 distinct personalities, people whose presences I intuit at a distance. That which teaches seems to inform me not to describe the episode too hurriedly but let it open like the sea creature…Big feelings are unsentimental. More than one idea sails past.

I have as yet no words about what emerges from the ink …

At the episode's finale I feel myself sinking back to "lesser consciousness." I only wish I could hold to what I am given and not fall back …

The Rat

Today's weapon of choice is a bamboo pole, the kind you normally find inside sod mats rolled up in a rug store.

In a Metropolitan episode I am out walking

without a leash when I see a pile of trash set out to be picked up near the corner. Amid the pile of mostly sticks and scraps, a large rat

slithers, almost cat-sized.

I am about to cross the street when I observe the old man with a cloth sack slung over his shoulder. He is a scavenger pawing through rubbish the way my uncle did for kindling in Construe ages ago. And the way I do now for the wood stove, sawing off dead Juniper branches on Forestry's hillside up behind my rental...The old man's sack makes me think of those burlap squares employed by garbage men long ago in Construe ...

If you live, when you have grown, the last thing you would ever want to be is a garbage man. In the playground somebody says, "My dad can beat your dad." So, if there is to be a prize fight, Ike versus Nikita, and neither side takes a dive, it's likely to decide the Cold War, once & 4all.

'cos they had a different system back then before green plastic trash bags and trucks with compactors...You pitched everything undifferentiated--coffee grounds, dead light bulbs--into beat-up galvanized cans in the garage. If the cans were emptied, there was often a greasy little puddle of flywater at bottom. And you knew when the garbage men were coming by a peculiar sound.

The sound, distant at first, growing louder

as they reached your street, was made by the feet of an iron ladder scraping against the road. The old dump trucks had an iron ladder hinged to the back that was flipped down when one slowed to enter a street where a collection was scheduled.

It seems to me now that there were 3 men per truck. A driver with 2 others to gather. In Construe the gatherers were usually black. If they didn't have much seniority, and consequently had been laid off at the mill, they might fill in in the interim, working while waiting to be rehired. The driver, who remained behind the wheel, could be black or white...Assuming a horse chestnut shaded the windshield, you might not have noticed without thinking about it.

I remember the way the 2 gatherers--in unbuckled black galoshes if it was winter--strode forward toward the garages. One to your house, one next door to the neighbors. If a can was full, the 4ft square of burlap was spread evenly on the pavement. The can was upended dumped and knocked into the center of the cloth. Each corner was then folded back toward the center to form a sack which was hoisted at once and slung over the shoulder. At the back, the gatherer hobbled rung by rung to the top of the iron ladder where the contents of the burlap were flung out into the rear of the truck. If it was not that heavy, only partly filled, the can itself was hauled one-handed up the ladder.

In summer, too, it seems to me, they wore unbuckled galoshes, which may have had to do with saving shoe leather where the contents of the truck were dumped. It might have been that the city owned the galoshes. In summer it would have been hot work. The faces of the gatherers, then, were glazed in beer sweat or plain sweat, depending on your interpretation. If there was a request for water at our back door, Elizabeth would hand out a glass milk bottle filled from the icy tap.

This was gratefully upended and polished off without further ado.

I remember a particular Sunday, call it Rat Sunday. The entire family, all 6 of us, were in the station wagon on the way home from churchgoing back in that ancient, Atlantean, churchgoing zone.

I think mother was driving. There was a white carnation pinned in father's buttohole in the church vestibule because he was an usher required to pass the collection plate. As the vehicle entered the garage she noticed and then we all noticed the busy nibbler next to the galvanized cans. A rat was not a usual occurrence in our suburban garage. While the rest of us remained seated, father in his Sunday best got out, took up a rusted garden hoe, cornered the fat vermin, and chopped it. The following Monday, mother would phone the fumigators who arrived with tanks of poison…The garage was sealed with tape and plastic and gas let in. We children were ordered never to go anywhere near the garage for 24hrs.

In the present episode, the old guy with the sack is a duped picker who, without noticing it, has gathered the rat into his bundle and is bearing it slung across his back.

A further development separates out the rat from the picker's bundle so that I can confront the creature face to face. That which cautioned me before about "blank check empathy" informs me today as I take hold of the bamboo pole and am about to slay the monster by shoving the pole down its throat. There is a moment when I almost demure, almost hesitate to shove the bamboo pole down a rat's throat and kill it. But, in the instant, I forget to hesitate, noticing that I have already skewered the rat, properly, and killed it …

The Rest of the Iceberg

I'm with my deceased father in a city. What city is not included. Since it contains a seminary, that would probably be Metropolis. The city remains unspecified as I lead him into the building. It's dark inside like a church. The windows seem framed as church windows, like a monochrome stained glass window illuminated in the 1933 how2draw I've been rereading.

Father asks about the seminary; is it an adjunct of a larger school? Barefoot--not comfortable within the absence of premeditation--I have to explain to him in what way the seminary remains an independant entity.

Inside the building, having lost my shirt, I am bare-chested. As before, at Rice Jungle, I am embarassed to find myself in a state of partial nudity. *What about* that garment of eternity? I notice others around, theological students, who by now I imagine must be fully invested.

The building resembles the city library I recollect from a summer job summer when I lived in the Shoebox Arms Htl., before moving downtown to a sublet on West 4th…The tiny pocket library that summer was located in the midtown section. There, in a dusty corner, I chanced upon an antique volume. The neat purple ink of its withdrawl slip indicated no one had borrowed the book for decades. Leafing through, the subject proved to be narrative technique. I remember obtaining another temp card to borrow it.

The seminary I associate with the library and the library with the how2, which characterized all possible narratives into, I think, 4 types. Stories based on the depiction of consistent character. Stories based on the depiction of consistent character. Stories based on conflicts between consistent characters. Stories based on volatile situations. Lastly, stories based on atmosphere. (There may have been a 5th category I don't recall.) Thinking again of these categories, it's as though I were anxious to memorize them for a trivial quiz rather than prepare for my final.

Though the battlefield be distanced, the "war" is nigh, and cold.

Flying Disc Versus the Neverending Traffic

"Under water, famine; under snow, bread."
--George Herbert (1593-1633)

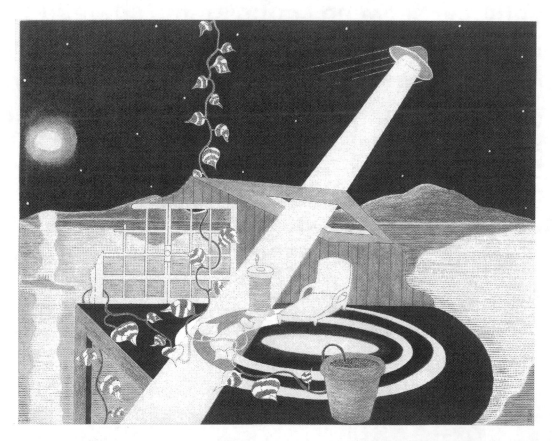

I'm with a group of kids, teenagers apparently. Two cars are parked close together as though preparing for a game of "chicken." Outside the vehicle I'm again kneeling to retie my cordovan when I happen to look to the sky, where I observe a flying saucer. It's angling down toward the ground at 20 degrees or so, moving quite slowly …

The sky is clear transparent blue. Bright sun. The saucer is aluminum-colored and reflects sunlight glintingly. It's shaped like an inverted TV dinner tray. There are indentations in the middle though it is round…It approaches the treed hilltop slowly …

When I look up I start to shout, "There's one! There's one!" because I've always wanted to see a saucer. Looking at it, it at first appears to be a flung hubcap but then, because of the indentations, like a TV dinner tray in in an ancient short story. I can see ordinary people standing outside, moving around on it, half-hidden behind the indentations. They don't resemble aliens from another planet. As they move around amid crenellations, I observe that they are wearing 2-toned, 1950s space uniforms. I assume the vehicle will land and it does, on the hilltop, where it soon disappears under snow, like a horseshoe crab scuttling under mud.

People near the top of the hill stare up as the saucer descends. Spellbound they wander, staring upward, out into the road…one of them so enthralled with sky she is smacked down by a truck …

Floundering, I begin to shout, "Watch it! Get out the road!"

Now the ground and road are snow-covered though it seems to me they were not when I first caught sight of 1vehicle. Already, snow has been packed down by neverending traffic. On the hilltop the saucer is invisible, having burrowed by means of whirring vibrations underneath snow.

Crossing A Street
In the Tin Boat

Like Nivon City, but not. Outside a parking garage I again face the street of neverending traffic…To enter across its stream, I resort to a little boat of tin. I have to pay a fare. I row across on dry land, then down the same semicircular driveway to a familiar building it turns out is not the 21st Century Club… This time, there is no delay. I immediately penetrate the structure through glass doors, passing instantly through darkened corridors to find myself standing in front of a glassed-in section.

Inside, in this instance, I see teachers, one sort of like RC, who I remember abandoned Bohemia without his degree, subsequent to reoccupying a subaltern position. I'm scheduled for an undivided interview, about to go in through glass doors for interrogation, when I notice I'm barefoot again. Sans freeboots

I feel intimidated. I can't remember the names of the others, presumably well shod, inside the office. I'm supposed to remember all their names and accomplishments, as if I were still captive and needing to pass an exam that is not mine. I'm about to submit to interrogation when I experience doubt I will ever be able to make a long-lasting impression …

Sub-Cloud Car

I get out of the transforming vehicle, newly morphed into taxicab, and am about to pay the driver when instead he hands me a bottle 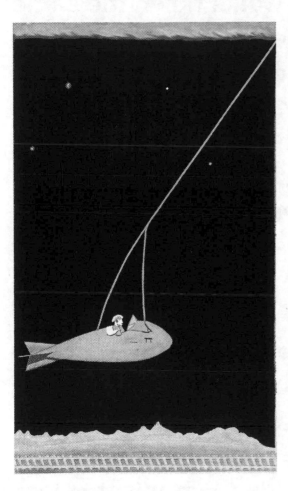 of rosé…bottle with a too wide cork. He explains the wine is home brew, concocted by yours truly. I don't know why a cab driver should be giving me a bottle of wine but remember that Italian gardener who once honored my father at Christmas with a bottle of his own home brew. This isn't that guy.

I've gotten out of the cab, smoking a big panatela, the way he used to do. No panzer ad attack. No unconscious blitz, so ideas surface as they are needed. Question of whether you just chew the end or bother with lighting it. Also, I am carrying a wooden salad bowl, empty, as though returning from a potluck dinner…Someone else walks down the same street. I recognize CG, fellow student I haven't laid eyes on for decades. He greets me and I say hello. There is no issue between us though he asks about these headphones I wear all the time now, to maintain context, since I have defined myself as "not an actor." For a lighthearted knee-slapper, I inform him, "I have communication with the mother ship above the clouds."

This must needs be a reference to the sub-cloud car, German W.W. I device their zeppelins used to winch down below cloud cover, from where an observer, wearing a telephone headset, could communicate clear coordinates to the bombardier overhead. I also imagine the cloud car might have been suspended selectively to teardrop spies into England.

I don't know exactly where the taxi has brought me or where this is leading. I have to admit, in the guise of my father as Beloved Vaudevillian, I invented the business about the mother ship.

When the cab driver presents me with wine I thank him. Although I no longer drink any myself, I explain I will pass it on to someone who does ...

Outdoors, sitting across the table from a hooded priest, a big chalice stands between us. I gaze into the chalice, observing wine, clarified except for a few specks, suspended and swirling slowly, as if recently stirred. I ask the priest if he did all the distilling himself. Of course, or course, he has distilled damn near a lake of the stuff. Then I have to ask for clarification--if he ever puts in any clay to absorb impurities.

The Value of Individual Memory

Cindy is showing me the sole of her left foot. There are two growths on it. One of them is a miniature lunar crater or volcano. It's reddish and seems inflamed. The other growth I'm not clear about, though it is neither reddish, nor inflamed. Somehow I'm involved in healing tiny growths which are like corns to be removed. Makes me think of the R. Lichtenstein painting of a giant foot based on a tiny illustrated sheet of instructions which used to be supplied with corn-removal ointment…except these growths are on her foot sole, not on her toes.

That other, positively extraneous details have gone missing is all I am given to dismember.

Printed in the United States
By Bookmasters